Taste of Marrow

ALSO BY SARAH GAILEY

River of Teeth

TASTE OF MARROW

SARAH GAILEY

A TOM DOHERTY ASSOCIATES BOOK
NEW YORK

This is a work of fiction. All of the characters, organizations, and events portrayed in this novella are either products of the author's imagination or are used fictitiously.

TASTE OF MARROW

Cover illustration by Richard Anderson
Cover design by Christine Foltzer

Edited by Justin Landon

A Tor.com Book
Published by Tom Doherty Associates
175 Fifth Avenue
New York, NY 10010

www.tor.com

ISBN 978-0-7653-9524-5 (ebook)
ISBN 978-0-7653-9525-2 (trade paperback)

First Edition: September 2017

For everyone who's ever carried me

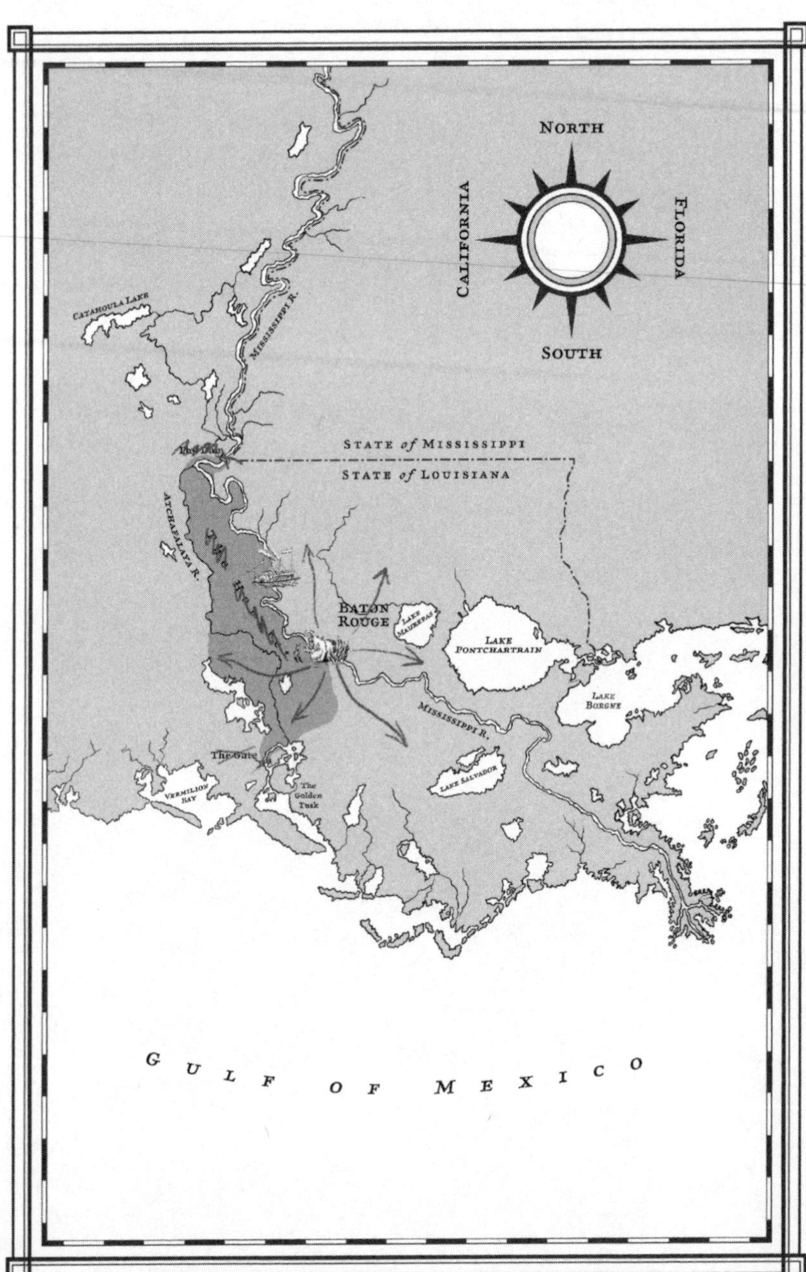
NORTH
CALIFORNIA
FLORIDA
SOUTH
CATAHOULA LAKE
MISSISSIPPI R.
STATE of MISSISSIPPI
STATE of LOUISIANA
ATCHAFALAYA R.
BATON ROUGE
LAKE MAUREPAS
LAKE PONTCHARTRAIN
LAKE BORGNE
MISSISSIPPI R.
The Gate
VERMILION BAY
The Golden Tusk
LAKE SALVADOR
GULF OF MEXICO

Taste of Marrow

Chapter 1

YSABEL WOULD NOT STOP CRYING. She spasmed with grating, earsplitting screams every few seconds. Her face, knotted and purple, jerked every time Adelia tried to maneuver her nipple toward the baby's mouth.

"Maybe she doesn't like you," Hero said mildly.

"Babies don't have opinions," Adelia replied through gritted teeth.

"Nobody told *her* that," Hero muttered. They turned their attention back to the kneeling saddle on the ground in front of them, and continued working grease into the leather of the pommel.

"Ysa," Adelia murmured in a pained singsong. "Ysa, mija, please just—*there.*" She winced, triumphant, as the screaming stopped and the baby latched at last. "You see? All she needed was—ah!" She cried out in pain as the baby startled at nothing in particular and pulled away from her breast without letting go of the nipple. Her cry made Ysabel startle again, and the baby's face began to scrunch in preparation for another piercing wail.

"Good luck with that," Hero said. They eased themself

upright, grimacing, and braced their hands on their lower back for a cautious stretch. They walked into the trees, away from Adelia and the screaming baby, without waiting to hear a response.

Hero knew that they'd need to start a fire soon, before dusk turned to dark. They'd wait until Ysabel had stopped eating—the sound of wood splintering was sure to startle the baby again. In the meantime, they made their way through the scrubby, moss-hung trees to the murky little pocket of the Catahoula where Adelia's hippos, Zahra and Stasia, were dozing. Hero squatted to wash their grease-smeared hands in the warm water, watching the surface of the pond for ripples more out of habit than worry. They watched the scum that floated away from their skin in the water and an idea drifted through their mind: a system to send rafts of nitroglycerin floating to waterlocked targets—but how to prevent a trailing wick from getting waterlogged? A remote detonator, or a system of watertight tubes that could protect a lit fuse, or perhaps a flaming dart shot across water, or perhaps . . .

They let their hands trail in the water for a while as they mentally troubleshot the concept. Hero couldn't remember the last time they'd allowed their attention to wander so close to the water's edge. But this was a safe place for them to let the ideas blossom. It was a pleasant, secluded little spot off the banks of the lake that Hero and Adelia had chosen to set up camp, well away from the Mississippi and the marshes and far from the reach of the ferals in the Gulf. Hero missed their Abigail—they'd been borrowing Stasia, and it just wasn't the same. But otherwise, it was a fine camp. They were surrounded by scrubby brush and gangly trees; it was out-of-the-way enough that no one was drawn to them by the sound of the baby crying. Hero wondered how far Ysabel's wails carried, and they allowed themself a moment of satisfaction at Adelia's struggle. *Serves her right,* they thought, ripping up a fistful of marsh grass to scrub their palms. Still, they couldn't help wishing that the baby was a little less of a squaller.

But not for Adelia's sake. It was just because Hero had to be stuck in the company of the little creature all day and all night, and their sanity was suffering from the constant barrage of noise.

Hero started to stand, but a flash of pain above their navel knocked them back and they sat hard. They yanked the hem of their shirt up and pressed a wet hand to the fat rope of scar tissue there, feeling for the unbroken skin. *There*—there was the scar, and they looked down at their hand and confirmed that no blood filled the creases in their palm. "It's okay," they whispered to themself. "It's okay. It's just a phantom pain. You're fine."

They sat there on the pebbly sand with their palm

braced against their belly. They *were* fine. But the "fine" was so *new*—this was the first day that Hero could truly say they felt healed, and even that was tentative, raw. The wound was relatively fresh, in more ways than one. It was the wound that Adelia had given to Hero just a few weeks before Ysabel's birth.

Hero took a slow, deep breath and took their hand away from their stomach, letting their hem fall back into place. In the distance, the baby had stopped screaming. A clutch of ducks drifted silently by on the water—a welcome signal that the ferals, who would have eaten anything that moved too slowly back on the Harriet, hadn't made it to the Catahoula yet. The night was almost peaceful now. Hero closed their eyes and tried to remember their last time they'd felt almost-peaceful—the day that a handsome man rode up to their door astride a pitch-black hippo and asked if they'd like to join him for one last job.

They'd said yes at the time. They would have said yes again in a heartbeat.

But Hero hadn't seen Winslow Houndstooth since the night before Adelia's knife had made that scar on their belly. Since her knife had nearly killed them.

Hero fidgeted with the third button down on their shirt. They wouldn't unbutton it to feel the scar there—the twin of the one on their stomach. *It hasn't dis-*

appeared since the last time you looked at it, they told themself irritably. But it bothered them, and they fidgeted in earnest as they went over the questions they'd been asking every day since they'd woken up.

It didn't make any sense.

Hero liked things that made sense. They liked diagrams and switches and sensible arrangements of wires. They liked dosages and measurements and titrations. Adelia was . . . a thicket. A tangle of intentions and motivations that Hero really could have done without.

But they had to figure it out. Adelia could have killed Hero so easily—but instead, her knives had struck the only places on Hero's body that could look mortal without actually killing them. Hero knew the exact amount of coral snake venom required to make a person quietly suffocate due to paralysis, and Adelia knew exactly where to aim her weapons. Both of them had too much experience to make stupid mistakes that would let a target walk away.

Hero knew that they'd been allowed to live intentionally. They just didn't know *why.*

Hero had woken up with no idea where they were, and there was Adelia, changing the bandage on their abdomen with steady hands and intent focus. Hero had tried to startle away from the woman who had stabbed them, but a white-hot stripe of pain had flattened them before they could move. It took them weeks to recover—weeks of Adelia's focused attention and care. Whenever Hero tried to ask why Adelia hadn't killed them, she pursed her lips and changed the subject.

And then Ysabel had come, and there hadn't been room to keep asking. And Hero had kept on healing, had kept on slowly recovering. They'd helped with the baby here and there, although they didn't know much of anything about babies and didn't care to learn. And the pain in their belly had faded.

Hero dug their hands into the coarse sand and watched the still surface of the water. The pain in their belly had faded, and Adelia had recovered from Ysabel's birth. It was time to leave. They knew it—had been thinking about it all day. They would tell Adelia that night, after the baby was asleep. It was settled. Hero would be gone by daybreak.

But where? Home? Back to their little house with its little pond, to be alone for the rest of their lives?

Because, if Hero was honest with themself, that was why they'd stayed with Adelia for so long. It was easy to focus on the wound in their belly and Ysabel's birth and the work of finding food and starting fires and staying two steps ahead of the law. It was easier for Hero to do all of that than it was for them to think about going home, sitting alone on the front porch, and looking at the empty rocking chair that Houndstooth should have been in. It was easier for Hero to do that than it was for them to wonder why it was that they'd survived the collapse of the Harriet dam, while Houndstooth—

No. *No,* they thought, slamming a door in their mind. *Don't think about that.* They turned their mind back to the problem of why Adelia hadn't killed them, and then realized how closely that question fit with the question they weren't going to think about. *Something else, anything else.*

They looked at the water, and gripped fistfuls of sand, and thought about how to keep a lit fuse dry. A sense of calm washed over them as they considered waxes and weights, how to keep the fuse from attracting fish, the problem of seepage, the problem of oxygen. And what if the fuse itself was on fire? Could they make it burn so hot that the water wouldn't matter?

They were drawing equations in the sand, calculating how many grams of gunpowder an inch of cotton wick could support—but then a scream cut through the muggy night air. Hero was used to screams cutting through all manner of night air at this point; sleeping a few feet away from a newborn baby will have that effect on a person. But this scream didn't sound at all like Ysabel.

It almost sounded like . . . *Adelia.*

Hero scrambled to their feet and pelted back toward the campsite. They slipped on a patch of loose scree, their leg shooting out behind them, but they caught themself and continued without breaking stride. Another scream—this one from Ysabel—and shouts, more than one person. "Shitshitshitshitshit," Hero chanted under their breath as they ran. They held one arm in front of their face to guard their eyes from twigs; with the other hand, they reached down to unstrap their fat-bladed kukri—usually reserved for utility, but it would do the job that needed to be done, whatever that job might be.

Except that it wasn't there. They groped at their hip even as they had a vision of the knife, sheathed, on the ground next to the kneeling saddle they'd been polishing. They would have sworn, but they were already swearing. "*Shitshitshit.*"

Hero burst into the little clearing where they'd left Adelia and Ysabel not fifteen minutes before. There was a resonant *thunk* next to their head—they looked, and saw the handle of a knife sticking out of a tree trunk less than a foot from their face. They pulled up short, their breath frozen in their throat.

Five men surrounded Adelia in a wide circle. Kerchiefs were tied over their faces, and their hats were pulled low, leaving only their eyes exposed. Adelia's outstretched right hand gripped the butt of Hero's kukri, and she turned in a slow circle, keeping the men at a distance and stepping around the empty sheath at her feet. In her left arm, a swaddled Ysabel whimpered steadily.

Hero's heart pounded in their chest so hard that it hurt. The odds in this situation were decidedly *not* in their favor. They weren't a fighter. They did poisons and explosives, the weapons of a thinking person. They had tolerable skill with a knife, theoretically, but against five people? They didn't stand a chance.

"Alright now, that's enough," one of the men said. "We ain't gonna hurtcha none, just—" Adelia swiped at him with Hero's kukri and he jumped back with a shout.

You don't have to fight, a small, reasonable voice whispered inside of Hero's mind. *You could just walk away from this.* Hero had been with Adelia for nearly two months. Adelia was more than recovered from Ysabel's birth. *You don't owe her anything,* the reasonable voice said. *You don't have to get involved in this at all.*

"I don't see why we can't hurt her a little bit," another of the men said. Blood seeped from a cut on his thigh. "Just knock her out, boss."

Hero took a slow, quiet step backward. They were good at being quiet—they could melt into the brush and no one would ever have to know that they'd been there at all.

"You knock her out, if you're so damn smart."

"Fuck that, she already cut me. You do it."

Hero took another step back. *You don't owe her anything,* the small voice whispered again.

"Jesus Christ, you two," a third man growled. "It's a woman and a baby." He shook his head at his colleagues, then lunged.

"No!" Hero heard the shout before they realized it was their own voice, and then they were running. They yanked the knife from the tree trunk with a back-wrenching tug, and then they were fighting.

It was exactly as awful as they'd feared. The men all looked the same, and even though Hero was certain they'd counted five before, it seemed like they were everywhere at once. Hero punched one of them in the gut, and another took his place right away. A fist connected with Hero's eye and everything went white, and then hot blood was getting into their eyes and they couldn't see anything. Hands grabbed at Hero's arms, and their pulse pounded in their ears, and they were being dragged away from Adelia. Ysabel was screaming. Adelia was cursing. Hero lashed out blindly behind themself with the knife and felt it catch on fabric and a man's voice near their ear said *agh hey watch it.* They lashed out again, and the knife caught on fabric again, and then they *pushed.*

The blade sank in with almost no resistance at all. The man who had said *watch it* made a sound like he was confused, or maybe startled. The grip on Hero's arms slackened, and they yanked themself free, wiping blood from their eyes with one sleeve. There was a meaty *thud* behind them, but they didn't stop to look, couldn't stop to look, because Adelia was shouting and the men were grabbing at Ysabel and the trees were shaking—

Wait, what? But before Hero could fully register their own confusion, the treeline exploded in a shower of leaves and loose moss, and three thousand pounds of damp, grey, furious hippopotamus thundered into the clearing. Zahra scattered the bedrolls under her close-set feet, barreling toward Adelia with all the momentum of a coal train. She knocked two of the masked men aside with a brutal shoulder check—one of them landed next to Hero with a splintering thud and didn't get up again.

Zahra's jaws gaped wide, revealing her cruelly sharp teeth, and she snapped at the remaining two men. The one farthest from the hippo turned to bolt and knocked hard into Adelia. The two of them fell in a tangle of limbs. The man's companion yanked him up by the arm and they both ran. One of the men Zahra had knocked over scrambled to his feet and followed them. Zahra started to charge after them, kicking up dry grass, but Adelia whistled sharply and the hippo trotted to a reluctant stop. She stood snorting at the place in the treeline where the men had disappeared, the vast grey expanse of her trunk heaving like a bellows.

"Adelia," Hero shouted, running to where she sat in the patchy grass of the clearing. "Adelia, are you alright? Where did he get you?" Adelia's breath was ragged, and she was clutching at the grass by her thighs with both fists. When she looked up at Hero, her face was clenched in naked agony. "Show me," Hero said, kneeling next to Adelia, not touching her but holding their hands a few inches from her shoulders as if they could shake the injury away.

But Adelia was shaking her head and tears were brimming in her eyes.

"Show me," Hero whispered. "I can help."

And then Hero realized that they could hear Zahra's huffing breaths, and they could hear the singing insects that were starting to come out as the sun went down. They could hear the groans of the man they'd stabbed. They could hear the crackle of dry grass under their own knees.

They could hear things they hadn't heard since Ysabel was born. For the first time in six weeks, it was quiet.

Hero stood up and scanned the entire clearing. "Adelia," they said, trying to keep their voice calm. "Where's Ysabel?"

Even as they said it—even before Adelia's anguished, furious scream split the night open—Hero knew the answer.

Ysabel was gone.

Chapter 2

"**NO ONE EVER SUSPECTS** the fat lady, hmmm?"

Regina Archambault whipped around to see who had whispered in her ear—but no one was there.

"Archie? Wassamatt'r?" The man Archie had been talking to a moment ago swayed toward her, his bourbon breath scalding her nostrils.

"Not a thing, chérie, not a thing." Archie placed a steadying hand on his shoulder, making the movement seem like a caress. The man—forty-something, white, all his teeth but none of his hair—looked down at her hand as though he were going to lick it.

"D'y'know," he said, casting a half-squinted eye at Archie's satin-swagged bosom, "that I'm the riches' man on the Pochnaroon?"

Archie pressed a hand to her chest, feigning surprise while tugging the neckline of her gown an inch lower. "Well, now, Mr. 'Aberdine, I never would 'ave guessed such a thing!" She gave Haberdine's bolo tie a tug, aimed a plump-lipped smile his way. "The richest man on the Ponchartrain, and so 'andsome as well? 'Ow could you keep this secret from me?" She pouted in the way a man like this would expect a Frenchwoman to pout. "I thought we were friends."

"It's not going to work."

That voice again, but this time Archie didn't turn to look at who it was. Whoever they were, they'd find her eventually. She wasn't going to play their game.

"I own"—Haberdine stifled a belch—"well, I *used't'own* all the boats on the Ponchatrawn and half th'ns on the Mississip, an' I tell you what, I—" He stopped midsentence, his eyes on Archie's leg. She'd reached into an inner pocket of her gown while he was talking, and she'd tugged on a strategically loosened string. A significant slit had opened up in the fabric, running from her calf to the top of her thigh.

"Tell me what," she whispered into Haberdine's ear, letting her leg edge toward him so that he could see the sheen of her stocking. His fingers trailed along the rent in the fabric. *Her* fingers trailed along the lining of his inner waistcoat pocket.

"Well, now, Ms. Archie—I was gonna say that if I thought I was rich before . . ." Haberdine licked his lips as his thumb traced the clasp of her garter where it met the top of her stocking. "T'ain't nothin' to how I'm set up now I've sold my boats."

"Sold them?" Archie murmured, tracing a fingertip

along his earlobe while feeling in his trousers for a billfold.

"Sol'm to Whelan Parrish, m'dear," Haberdine said. "Why, that boy's buying up all the property he can get a *handful* of—"

Archie jumped prettily, and Haberdine chuckled. "Oh, mon dieu, Mr. 'Aberdine, I—"

"Who's your friend, Marcus?"

Haberdine snatched his hand out from under her skirt. Archie's lightning reflexes, honed over a lifetime of grift, were the only thing that saved her from dropping his wallet on the ground between them. She slipped the wallet into a pocket in her bustle as she turned to see who Marcus was sweatily eyeing.

"Marcus, my love, I've been looking for you everywhere." There was no mistake to be made—it was the same voice as the one that had been taunting Archie all night, from the moment she'd "bumped into" Haberdine on the dance floor to the first drink he'd bought for her. The young woman belonging to the voice was, in many ways, Archie's opposite. Where Archie was pale, she was dark; where Archie was broad as a pistol's grip, she was thin as a knife's edge; where Archie's hair was piled in a tower of blond ringlets, this woman's was close-cropped and glossy, set in immaculate waves. But there was something more there. Where Archie was tired, this woman's skin seemed to glow.

Where Archie was enjoying playing with Haberdine, this woman's eyes spoke to hunger. This wasn't a game to her.

"Cayja," Haberdine slurred, grinning at this new woman. "I was jus' talkin' business with this'r upstanding lady. Meet Ms. Archie—er, Archie . . ."

"Just Archie is fine," Regina said, extending a hand.

"Acadia," the other woman drawled, ignoring it. "Marcus, dear heart, we had probably better get back to our boat."

"But th'party's just getting started!" he said, gesturing expansively to the crowd that surrounded them. He was right—their party boat, just like every other one that floated on the surface of the Ponchartrain, was packed with shouting, dancing, drunk people, and the crowd was growing livelier by the minute. "In fact, I could use a refill—" And with that, Haberdine gracelessly excused himself from the company of both women.

"I am sorry," Archie said, "I didn't know that 'e was spoken for—"

"Git," Acadia said through gritted teeth. Her fists were clenched in the full pink skirt of her gown, and Archie could see her holding back a formidable anger.

"Pardonnez-moi?"

"I said *git,*" Acadia spat, something like fear glinting in her eyes, and Archie revised her earlier assessment. This wasn't a woman. This was a girl *dressed up* as a woman.

"Are you alright?" Archie asked softly, remembering other times she'd met desperate young women wearing pearls that older women had loaned them. "Is 'e—are you safe 'ere?"

Acadia stepped closer to Archie, glancing around them before she answered. "Well . . . I suppose maybe I can trust you . . ."

Archie bent her head to listen. "Of course, chérie."

Acadia's lips brushed Archie's ear at the same time as a needle-sharp knife pricked her hip. "This is my grift, Regina Archambault." Her voice was low, husky, a shade above a whisper but more intimate for it. Her breath was hot on Archie's throat. "That man just sold his empire, and I've been working on him for a fucking month, and the fortune he's sittin' on is *mine*. So *git*."

Archie nodded. "I see. Thank you for letting me know." She put a fingertip on the girl's knife and pushed it away from her abdomen. "It is as I said: I did not realize 'e was spoken for. I'll take my work elsewhere."

"To another boat," Acadia said. "There are plenty here. This one's mine."

Archie nodded. She couldn't help respecting the girl's work—after a few hours in Haberdine's company, she'd been tempted to pitch him overboard. A full month . . . the girl would be earning her fortune. "'Ave a pleasant evening," Archie said. The girl gave her a curt nod, and with that, they parted ways.

Archie smiled to herself as she paid one of the Ponchartrain gondoliers a penny to ferry her back to the *Marianna Fair*. It had been a good night, even if she'd been called away. She reached into one of the pockets of her skirt, the one where she'd slipped Haberdine's wallet before being so rudely interrupted. The wallet was fat, ripe with bills—likely his advance on the sale of his empire.

She felt in the pocket again.

There was a rustle of paper there. Thick, heavy stock, debossed or imprinted with something. She pulled the paper out, held it up to the gondolier's lantern, and laughed.

It was a calling card. The girl had left a card in Archie's pocket—nervy as hell, that one. She felt around in the pocket again, and realized that, while the wallet was still there, the two watches she'd lifted from other marks that night were gone.

"Well earned, Acadia," she laughed to herself, studying the calling card. "I'll 'ave to be in touch with you, eh?"

For the rest of the trip between the party boats and the *Marianna Fair,* Archie watched the water. Strictly speaking, she shouldn't be worried—the ferals hadn't made it as far as the Ponchartrain yet, at least according to all the latest accounts. They wouldn't like the brackish, choppy waters of the lake. It was why there were so many people on the water even this late in the season—everyone was congregating in places they thought the ferals were avoiding.

Still, Archie watched the water. She flinched every time a ripple crossed the surface.

~

Archie eased open the door of the suite she was sharing with her old friend, tiptoeing so as not to wake him. But when she got inside, she found him standing at the little desk that took up half their room, working by the light of a single gas lantern.

"I'm just—hang on," Houndstooth said distractedly, waving a hand at Archie without looking up.

Archie sighed, unclipping her skirt and tossing it on the bed before pulling on a pair of well-worn breeches. She didn't bother trying to tuck herself behind a screen—Houndstooth was too wrapped up in his work to notice her partial nudity. She needled him, even though she knew he wouldn't listen. "You should go to sleep, Winslow. It must be two o'clock in the morning, my friend."

The only response she got was the sound of his grease

pencil smudging across the map, and the lapping of water against their boat. She frowned at Houndstooth. He was bent over the tiny desk, a long parenthesis in the flickering light of the gas lantern. Archie tutted. She didn't care to be ignored. She turned away from Houndstooth, bumping into furniture on her way to the washbasin. She loosened her corset, washed her face, took out her false curls, began putting her hair up into the crown of braids she'd be sleeping in. She could see the entirety of the little room in the palm-sized mirror that hung on a nail over the washbasin: the narrow bed, the narrower chair, the postage stamp of a desk. The little window that wouldn't open to let in the salty breeze coming off the lake.

Houndstooth was muttering something under his breath. Archie pursed her lips, tying a silk scarf over her braids. She set her hands on her hips and turned to stare at him.

"Houndstooth," she said.

"If they followed the currents," Houndstooth muttered. "But—no, that wouldn't be—no, no, damn it." His elbows arrowed out as he pushed his hands through his hair. For a moment, Archie thought he'd turn around and acknowledge her, but he just bent back over the map. She put a hand on his shoulder and he startled.

"Archie—what are you doing up?" He finally looked at her. "Where have you been in that dress?"

"I've been obtaining us travel funds," she said. "'Oundstooth, you look terrible. You need to rest."

He laughed. "Well, thanks, Archie, that's very sweet of you."

Archie laid a palm against Houndstooth's cheek. He felt warmer than he should have. "I think you are not well, perhaps. Please, my friend. Get some sleep. I'll take the chair for the rest of the night. You take the bed." It was a generous offer—the chair was narrow enough for Houndstooth to sleep in, but it was far too small for Archie. She knew that if he took the bed, she would spend half the night trying to find a way to squeeze herself comfortably between the carved wooden arms—but that didn't matter. Not with Houndstooth blinking back at her as if he barely recognized her. *Maybe he'd talk to me more if I was a gull-damned* map, she thought bitterly.

"I can't sleep, Archie," Houndstooth said. His eyes were bright, but they were rimmed with shadows. Archie frowned at him, and his shoulders drooped. He whispered, "I can't sleep while Hero is missing."

Archie rubbed her forehead so that Houndstooth would not see her rolling her eyes. *So melodramatic.* "You can't find them if you're exhausted," Archie replied, shaking her head. "Please. Just . . . rest until sunrise. I'll wake you up then." She patted his cheek a little harder than necessary. "I promise."

Houndstooth glanced at the bed, and Archie could see the battle between the physical need for rest and the pull of his—she mentally elided the word "obsession." She nudged him toward the bed. "I swear on Rosa's head, mon amie. I'll wake you at sunup."

"Alright," he muttered, "but only because I know you won't let me concentrate anyway." He stretched out on top of the covers, his bloodred hippo-leather boots hanging off the end of the bed. Archie turned the gaslamp down until it was dark in the little cabin.

She tried to settle into the chair and sighed. It dug painfully into the sides of her thighs. She shifted, but she knew that it wasn't an issue of her position—the chair was just too damned small. Damn if her thighs wouldn't be bruised later. She folded her hands over her stomach and closed her eyes, determined to try to sleep in spite of the nagging discomfort of the chair. She listened to Houndstooth's breathing slow down, and she listened to the gentle lapping of the waters of Lake Ponchartrain against the side of the boat, and she tried hard to doze off—but it was no good. She was too worried about Houndstooth.

When did it happen? Archie asked herself. She couldn't pinpoint the exact moment when her old friend had gone from *determined* to *fixated*. He'd always been stubborn, always a little . . . performative. But it seemed like he'd crossed a line somewhere.

When the Harriet Gate fell and the Harriet Dam blew, they hadn't known that Hero was missing. Hurt, yes—but not *missing*. They hadn't known Hero was *missing* for nearly a day—the amount of time it took them to escape the Harriet, dodge the ferals that had been released into the river, and find the doctor that Hero had been taken to.

The doctor they had been taken to by U.S. Marshal Gran Carter.

Archie's hand crept to the inside pocket of her shirt, where she'd tucked Carter's latest letter. It was too dark to read it, and if she unfolded it Houndstooth would wake up, thinking that she was interfering with his map. But that was okay—she didn't need to look at it. She'd memorized it.

I miss you. I want to see you again. I miss the way you smell. I miss the way you taste. I'll be on Ponchartrain in a fortnight, aboard the Marianna Fair. *Meet me there, and we can—*

Archie's eyes snapped open. Was that—no. She'd thought for a moment that she'd heard a splash, but it had probably just been the water lapping against the side of the boat. She reminded herself for the hundredth time that the lake was safe. Houndstooth made a soft sound in his sleep, a bad-dream sound, and Archie closed her eyes again. She tried to slow her breathing. She would need to sleep so that she could get Houndstooth through the next day of searching for Hero. She had never seen him like this before—she had to remind him to eat, to drink water, to comb his hair . . .

This time, Archie stood from the chair before she knew what she was doing. There had *definitely* been a splash, and a scream. She pressed her face to the window, trying to see through the streaky glass, but she couldn't make out what was happening on the lake. There was another scream, closer, and then a sound that made the bottom drop out of Archie's gut: the grating bellow of a feral's roar.

"Putain," she whispered. "Son of a bitching *fuck*. Houndstooth—!"

"Let's go," he said. She turned around and he was already standing behind her, one hand gripping the waxed leather saddlebag that held the majority of their possessions. He reached past Archie to grab the map he'd been scribbling on. Archie grabbed her jacket from the back of the chair and whipped it on as they left their room. The hall was strangely silent.

"Where's everyone else?" Archie asked Houndstooth's back.

"They probably haven't woken up yet. Or they don't know," he called over his shoulder. "I don't think there are any other hoppers on board."

Archie hesitated. "Couillon," she muttered again. She banged on the door closest to them with the flat of her hand and didn't stop until the door swung open. A grey-faced man answered, and Archie grasped him by the lapels of his nightshirt. "Listen," she said, her nose a half-inch from his. "There are ferals in the water. They'll kill everyone here, and this boat is small enough for them to flip over. Everyone on board needs to get to shore immediately and then run inland. Do you understand?"

"But—how—" the man sputtered. "Who are you?"

She slapped him. Not as hard as she could, but as hard as he needed to be slapped. "Wake up the others," she said, gesturing to the two other doors in the hall. "Get their help waking the crew downstairs, and then get to shore before the ferals get here. If you want to live, it's what you'll do. Do you understand?" The man hesitated, and Archie lifted her hand again.

"I understand!" he cried, holding his hands up in front of his reddening cheeks. "But—where are you going?"

But Archie was already gone, tearing down the stairs after Houndstooth. Behind her, she could hear the man starting to knock on doors. *Good.*

By the time she and Houndstooth reached the main deck, the screams were constant. The moon provided just enough light to see shadows in the water—some moving, some not. There was a fire, and Archie thought it was probably the wreckage of a houseboat or maybe a skiff that had anchored for the night. The grunting of the ferals was everywhere.

Houndstooth dug around in the saddlebag and hauled out Archie's meteor hammer. She gave it a couple of practice swings as Houndstooth strapped a knife to each of his arms.

"Winslow," she said urgently, staring across the water at the silhouettes of the ferals. "The harpoon. If there's ever been a time—"

He shook his head. "I haven't practiced with it. I'll row, you just . . . try not to hit me with the hammer, eh?"

"Then *I'll* use it," she snapped, and then took matters into her own hands. She reached into the saddlebag, pulled out four lengths of cylindrical brass, and started latching them together.

"Archie, we don't have time to—"

"If you die trying to get off the water, we'll never find Hero," Archie said. "And my hammer might hit the raft, it's no good out here. Where's the head? Never mind," she said, digging into the saddlebag again. "I've got it." She pulled out a notched spearhead the size of her forearm and attached it to the end of the long pole. She fumbled—she wasn't used to putting the damn thing together, and she kept startling as people screamed and ferals bellowed and wood splintered—but then she felt a satisfying *snick* and she knew that the head was secure. "Alright," she said, "let's go. You steer."

Houndstooth stepped over the railing of the *Marianna Fair* onto the raft that was tethered there—the raft on which he and Archie had arrived just a few nights before. He held it steady as she lowered herself slowly onto it. The roaring of the ferals came closer, and the process of shifting ballast to the center of the raft was taking too long, but if Archie was going to be on the back of the raft with the harpoon and Houndstooth was going to be on the front of the raft with the pole—they couldn't capsize. Of this, Archie was certain: falling into the water meant death.

Finally, *finally,* they were ready, and Houndstooth lowered a long pole into the water and pushed off. They were moving slowly, trying not to attract the attention of the ferals. Ripples spread across the water in front of them and behind, and Archie watched the black surface of the lake, waiting for a single ripple that moved in the wrong direction.

She looked up at the shore. It seemed so far. Houndstooth let out a grunt of effort, and Archie felt a pang of sympathy—his wounds from their battle on the Harriet probably hadn't fully healed yet. She glanced over her shoulder at him, and she thought she saw his silhouette tremble.

She almost didn't hear the splash next to the raft. Almost.

She looked down and saw a ripple in the water, the front of a wake that started a hundred yards away. Archie yelled and pulled back the harpoon. An instant later, a feral's head burst out of the water, teeth bared, nostrils flared and blowing water. The feral bellowed, a bone-rattling roar, its mouth gaping like a bear trap. It snapped at the raft, its jaws closing inches from the place on the platform's edge where Archie's foot was braced. Archie lunged with the harpoon. The hippo roared again, and Archie put all of her considerable weight behind her weapon as she drove it through the roof of the beast's mouth. The sharp head of the harpoon drove through the feral's skull like a pitchfork sinking into a rotted log, and Archie yanked back hard before it pierced the other side of the animal's head. The harpoon jumped back into her hand, slippery with blood and saliva; lakewater and gore filled the feral's mouth, black in the moonlight.

Archie's momentum nearly knocked her flat—but then Houndstooth gave a mighty shove with his pole, and the raft jumped forward. The feral—dead, surely it was dead—started to sink beneath the surface of the lake; but then, as Archie watched, it bobbed back up to the surface. Archie swore under her breath—she must not have gored it deeply enough in the brain. She wiped one hand at a time on her breeches, trying to get a good grip on the blood-slick shaft of the harpoon, ready for another attack.

The feral twitched in the water.

Then, as she watched, it jerked beneath the surface.

Archie swore again and looked past the feral—it was hard to see in the water, and they were moving away from the beast as quickly as Houndstooth could row. But she was sure that she could see more ripples. She glanced up at the sky, which was just starting to lighten, and cursed the sun for taking so long to rise. She looked back down at the water and—yes, there, ripples, those were *definitely* ripples.

Her suspicion was confirmed a moment later as two more ferals burst up out of the water. They roared at each other as they fought over the carcass of their late fellow.

Archie nearly fell off the raft as it shuddered. She shouted, raised the harpoon, certain that a feral had gotten under the raft and was about to tip them over—

"Archie, we're here! It's the shore!" Houndstooth was yelling behind her. "You get off first, I have to brace us!"

Archie started to argue, but then she saw one of the ferals near the carcass of the one she'd killed raise its head. She was certain it was looking toward the sound of Houndstooth's shouting—and then it disappeared beneath the surface of the water.

"Fils de pute," she said, then jumped off the raft and

into the shallows. Houndstooth's side of the raft dipped into the water, threatening to capsize. He tossed Archie the saddlebag as she waded to shore before jumping off the raft himself. They ran to shore, their legs frothing the water, and kept running. They didn't stop, not even at the sound of the *Marianna Fair* splintering. Not at the sounds of screams in the water. Not at the sound of their raft shattering under the jaws of the feral that had chased them to shore. They kept running inland toward the freshwater paddock, toward Ruby and Rosa. They kept running until it was light out and they could be sure that they were too far for the ferals to chase them overland.

They kept running until they were far enough from the carnage that they could no longer smell the blood in the water.

Chapter 3

THE UNCONSCIOUS MAN LOOKED small and soft without the bandana tied over his face.

Adelia squatted beside the man and studied him. He was a stubbly, tan, nose-broken type. His mouth hung slack, and Adelia could see his little pink tongue in there, flopped over to one side.

She had always been struck by how soft people were. They could throw punches, sure, but at the end of the day, they were a mess of vulnerabilities. This man's face had been covered in an attempt to protect himself from Adelia's inevitable retribution—and yet he'd yielded to Hero's clumsy jab. Hero was bad at fighting; Adelia had been astonished that they had managed to land a blow.

But then, Adelia reminded herself, people could be surprising.

Ysabel had been surprising. Adelia had expected to love the baby, to cherish and nurture her—but she could never have anticipated how much she *liked* Ysabel. It usually took Adelia months to warm up to people, and yet the moment that Ysabel was born, Adelia had felt as if they'd been best friends for years.

Go figure.

Adelia felt a faint smile shade her lips at the thought of her daughter's eyes staring up at her, wide and dark and just like her own. She smiled that little smile in spite of the gut-clenching terror: *Those men have Ysabel.* She smiled because she knew what to do with this man, this man who had helped to steal her baby.

She drew back her hand, and she slapped the unmasked man across the face, with approximately one-tenth of the force that her rage demanded.

He came to, spitting blood. He coughed, gagged, started to choke. Hero shoved him upright and slapped him on the back, and he coughed again, then spat something white. Adelia picked it up.

"You lost this," she said, showing the man his tooth. He breathed hard through his nose as he poked at his gum with his tongue. He spat blood again, then looked from Hero to Adelia with wide, spooked eyes.

"What's your name?" Adelia asked softly. Hero stood behind the man, fidgeting with their shirttails. Adelia smiled at them. They winced. Adelia supposed that her smile was not very reassuring at the moment—not while she was holding a bleeding man's tooth.

Oh, well. If he had wanted to keep all of his teeth, he would not have helped those men steal Ysabel.

"You—you *bitch,* my *tooth,* you—"

Adelia dropped the man's tooth on the ground and grabbed him by the chin. In one hand, she gripped his lower jaw, prying it open. With the other, she reached into his mouth and grasped the tooth just behind his right canine—the companion to the one he'd already lost. She gripped it between her thumb and forefinger and gave an experimental tug. The man made a throaty howling sound, and she extracted her hand from his mouth.

"Qué?" she asked pleasantly. "I didn't catch that."

"My name's Feeney," the man panted. "Doug Feeney."

"Ah, excellent! It is nice to make your acquaintance, Doug Feeney," Adelia said. Then, before he could sag with relief, she grabbed his jaw again. He choked in surprise, his eyes popping. Adelia felt that ghost of a smile again, a kind of comfort warming her fingertips. Yes. She knew exactly what to do with this man.

Having a child hadn't made her forget her craft, and it certainly hadn't taken the edge off her speed.

She reached into his mouth and found the tooth she'd tugged on before. As Doug Feeney let loose a gargling screech, she gave a sharp twist of her wrist. She wrenched her elbow back, and with a rich, wet crack, Doug's tooth ripped free of his jaw.

Adelia rocked back onto her heels as Doug spat blood

and whimpered. She picked up the tooth that she had dropped onto the ground, and rattled the pair in her cupped palm like dice. "There," she said. "Now you match."

Near the treeline, Hero was retching. Adelia held in a *tch*. She had known that Hero was thin-skinned, but this was ridiculous. It was only a tooth, after all. He had plenty more.

"So, Doug Feeney," Adelia said. "Who sent you?" He opened his mouth to answer, and Adelia held up a warning finger. "Don't lie to me." She tossed one of his teeth into the air and caught it on her fingertip. It was easy—like catching the blade of a knife point side down—but the man gaped anyway, blood and drool running out of his open mouth. "If you lie to me, things will not be pleasant for you."

"Adelia," Hero said. "I don't know if—"

Adelia looked at Hero patiently. Hero swallowed, then looked away. "What is it, Hero?" Adelia said, careful to keep her voice kind. She wanted to hear what Hero had to say. She really did.

"I just don't know if we can believe what he says," Hero said. "What's to keep him from steering us wrong?"

Adelia looked from Hero to the man on the ground. "Are you going to lie to me, Doug Feeney?" she asked. "Are you going to 'steer me wrong'?"

He shook his head vehemently, then spat blood onto the ground. It wasn't that much blood—he was being dramatic. Adelia tutted. "In my pocket," Feeney said. "Just look in my pocket, it's right—no, not that one—" Adelia had already shoved him hard, forcing him to lie down. She began to turn his pockets inside out with the quick efficiency of a woman who had searched more than her fair share of unconscious men for information. A folding knife fell to the ground, and she placed it in the center of Feeney's chest along with a pocket watch, a handful of peanut shells, and a smooth rock. Oh, and Feeney's teeth. Those went on his chest too, right where he could see them. Finally, she found a crumpled paper, limp with the humid sweat of the man's pockets.

She handed the paper off to Hero for safekeeping, then picked up the smooth rock. "What's this for?" she asked.

Feeney stammered and tried to sit up. Adelia pressed the tip of her index finger to his forehead, keeping him supine. She liked him better that way. "I, uh, I—it's a souvenir." The tip of his tongue poked out to wet his lower lip where it had split under Adelia's slap. "I'm not from around here, and whenever I travel I try to bring a little something home for my boy."

"How old is your boy?" Adelia asked. Her eyes were locked on the man's dilated pupils. He seemed unable to look away from her, even at the sound of Hero tearing open the letter. His breath came fast and shallow. *They sent a lamb,* Adelia thought. *They sent prey to hunt me down.* She returned the rock to Feeney's chest and picked up the pocket knife. She opened it, examined the blade.

"He's five," Feeney whispered. "Please don't kill me. He's five."

Please don't kill me. How many times had Adelia heard those words? She had always been very good at ignoring them, but something was different now.

It wasn't Ysabel. Ysabel was . . . "symptom" wasn't the right word. She was a by-product of this softening, a piece of the emerging puzzle that was life after retirement. The desire to have Ysabel had come after Adelia had decided that she was done killing, after her last job in California had gone so wrong, nearly a year before.

Not wrong. Right. It had gone perfectly, and five men had been dead before she'd so much as blinked. Five men dead, and her heartbeat hadn't so much as stuttered. That had begun the shift—a feeling that she needed to stop the work she'd spent a lifetime perfecting. A certainty that it was time for a change.

She still wasn't sure that she liked the change.

"I wasn't going to kill you," she murmured, still examining the man's knife. "But thank you for asking so nicely."

Feeney started to sob as Adelia took up Hero's

kukri—a fat, heavy knife, better suited to hacking through underbrush or dislocating joints than to the fine grade of work Adelia preferred—and began honing the blade of the folding knife against it. She used short, quick strokes. The Adelia of a year ago would have used long strokes, theatrically long ones, slow and grating. She would have watched with detached satisfaction as Feeney grew hypnotized with terrified anticipation. But it wasn't a year ago, and Adelia wasn't interested in Feeney's terror. The adrenal hunger of knowing that this man had helped steal Ysabel hadn't worn off, but its edge was gone, and now Adelia just felt tired. It was the same fatigue she'd felt throughout the hippo caper on the Harriet, as Travers had endlessly wheedled her and blackmailed her and threatened her.

She was so tired.

"Adelia, you should read this," Hero was saying, but Adelia shook her head.

"Momento," she said. "I'm almost finished." She sheathed her fat knife and picked up the smooth stone from Feeney's chest, then rose from her crouch to face Hero. "Qué onda?"

"This is a letter for you," Hero said. They held out the paper, but Adelia didn't take it. Her hands were occupied; she scratched at the smooth stone with the folding knife, not looking up.

"And?"

"It, um." Hero faltered. "It's a ransom letter, sort of. It says that if you want Ysabel back you have to go to Baton Rouge and get her."

Adelia glanced at Feeney, whose face had taken on the glazed look of a man who couldn't process any more fear. She nudged him with her foot. "Feeney. If I go to this place, will I be ambushed and killed?"

"No," he breathed. "Not that they told me, anyway. They just said to get the baby and leave the letter, though, so . . . maybe."

"Hmph." Adelia turned back to her etching on the smooth stone. "Alright, so, we'll go there." She paused. "*I'll* go there. My apologies, Hero. I did not mean to presume."

Hero remained silent, and Adelia allowed herself a small internal sigh as she dropped the stone into her shirt pocket. She had no right to expect Hero's forgiveness. Even if it had been a coup to make the injuries seem grave while avoiding any mortal wounds, she'd still stabbed Hero. She'd still made them feel pain and fear and the terrible loneliness that comes with waking up in a strange place with strange injuries.

It had been nice to have company, though. While it had lasted.

Adelia crouched beside Feeney and held the blade of

his folding knife where he could see it, very close to his eyes. The glazed look on his face gave way to renewed fear, and he began to blubber again. Adelia tapped the flat of the blade against his lips.

"Shhh," she said. "Listen." He went silent as she held the blade up in front of his eyes again. "You need to take better care of your knives. Whet the blade every so often, especially if you're going to leave it folded up all the time in your sweaty pocket. And oil this hinge, sí?" She turned the knife so he could see the little flakes of rust building on the place where the knife folded. "This is a good blade and it could last you a long time. You could pass it down to your son someday, if you take good care of it."

Feeney didn't nod—smart of him, with the tip of the knife so very close to his eyes. But he licked his lips and whispered, "I will. I'll take better care of it."

"Good," Adelia said. She folded the blade and tucked it back into the pocket it had fallen out of. Then she did the same with the other detritus on Feeney's chest—even the peanut shells. She held up his teeth, examining them, and then put one into his shirt pocket. The other she dropped into her own shirt pocket, winking at the horrified man as it clicked against the stone that was in there. "Just in case," she said. "If that letter is a trick, I'll come back to get the matching one."

Finally, Adelia untied the rope from Feeney's wrists

and coiled it, hanging it on her belt. She could have simply cut him loose, but it wouldn't do to waste good rope.

Don't kill me, he'd said. It kept echoing in Adelia's mind. *Please don't kill me.*

Feeney scrambled to his feet, and Adelia grabbed his arm, preventing him from running away. He so clearly wanted to run away.

"Here," she said, pulling the smooth stone from her shirt pocket and putting it in Feeney's hand. "This will be a better souvenir for your son than a plain stone. Now, he'll always know where it came from. He'll prefer that, don't you think?"

The man turned the stone over in his hand to see Adelia's etching of a hippopotamus. Its mouth gaped to show fearsome fangs, and a little bird was perched on its nose. Adelia thought it was quite good.

Feeney didn't say anything. He closed his fist around the stone, looked between Hero and Adelia, and then bolted into the trees.

Adelia sighed. The boy would like the stone, especially if his father told him the story of its provenance. He would probably carry it around in his pocket until the day he died.

She nodded at Hero, then took the letter from them and studied it. Hero hadn't left out anything but the signature line—Whelan Parrish, a name Adelia had hoped she'd never have to hear again. She quickly committed his words to memory before folding the paper and tucking it into the sheath of the knife on her thigh for safekeeping. She rested a hand on Hero's shoulder as she passed them.

"Thank you," she said.

"For what?" Hero asked, glancing down at Adelia's hand.

"For trying to help," Adelia said. "You could have run, but you didn't. I know you're not a fighter—I'm sure that it was very frightening to run into the middle of that fight. I . . ." Adelia realized that she'd started journeying through her thanks without a destination in mind. "Thank you for trying," she finished clumsily. She walked away before Hero could answer.

As Adelia headed to the pond to begin preparing Zahra for the trip to Baton Rouge, she took a mental inventory. It would be a one-week ride at the minimum. She had her bedroll and supplies, and a bag of Ysabel's swaddling cloths, but only enough food to ride for a few days without stopping for provisions. She considered her options: the food might last just long enough if she cut herself down to half rations, but she had been ravenous since Ysabel was born. She made a mental note to buy more food at the earliest opportunity, although it would mean spending the last of her money. She cursed herself for not stealing anything from Houndstooth or Travers before fleeing the Harriet. She had her weapons—mostly small blades, since those had been easiest to wield during her pregnancy, but she'd hung on to her best machete just in case. She wondered if perhaps she should sell it, just to give herself a bigger financial cushion for the journey.

Some distant part of Adelia's mind raised concerns about her priorities. She should be wailing and tearing her hair out and then lying on the floor for weeks, refusing food and water, mute with unspeakable grief. She should be nurturing the beginnings of a lifetime of wounded rage—not mentally cataloguing which of her knives was the most valuable. *Mama would be so disappointed in me,* Adelia thought, remembering the many times that her mother had slapped her tearless face.

And yet, as she waded into the water up to her waist and began checking Zahra's teeth and feet and underbelly, making sure that she was prepared for the long journey ahead, Adelia could not find anger within herself. She had never been able to find anger—not the kind of anger her mother had specialized in, anyway. Adelia could be angry at a distance; she could feel the nagging discomfort of *wrongness,* and the desire to fix it. She could be angry in the moment, when a flush of adrenaline drove her at her opponent. But she could not find within herself the sustained outrage that she was certain she ought to feel. She was not angry that Ysabel had been taken; it was simply a problem.

A problem that she was going to fix.

When she was satisfied that Zahra was in good shape for a long ride, Adelia sprinkled the hippo's broad grey back and sides with white resin, to keep the padded underside of the saddle from slipping around and giving Zahra blisters. She heaved her kneeling saddle up onto Zahra's back with a grunt—she had always been strong, but something had slipped out of place during her long labor, and lifting the heavy saddle wasn't as easy as it used to be. She secured the saddle over Zahra's back and patted her girl on the flank. "I'll be right back, Zita." Zahra grumbled a little, and Adelia rolled her eyes as the hippo presented her broad, flat nose insistently. "I have spoiled you," she said, scratching under Zahra's chin. The hippo grumbled again and pushed at Adelia with her nose until Adelia planted a kiss on the tip of it. This finally satisfied the beast, and Adelia was allowed to leave the pond without comment.

She dripped her way back through the trees to the camp. When she emerged from the treeline, she saw immediately that Hero's bedroll and saddlebags were gone. *That was fast,* she thought with dismay. She found Stasia settled under a tree, eyes half lidded. She wondered how Hero was planning to haul the saddlebags without a hippo to ride. She had known, from a few comments that

Hero had made and from the way their eyes watched the horizon, that they had been planning to leave her soon. Still . . . it stung her. *I would have given them Stasia,* she thought. *If they had just asked.*

Adelia pulled up short as she walked farther into the little clearing and saw that her own bedroll was gone as well. And her saddlebags—everything. All of it was gone.

She reached for the knife at her side and turned in a slow circle, shifting her weight onto the balls of her feet and bending her knees into a familiar defensive stance. There was a rustle at the treeline a few feet from her, and she twisted, pulling her arm back to throw her knife at the figure that was emerging there—

"I think I've got everything packed up," Hero said, wiping their hands on their trousers, "but you'll probably want to take one last look around before we—" They looked up, and their eyes went round as they took in Adelia, who had frozen in the instant before releasing her knife. They looked over their shoulder, then back at Adelia. "What are you doing?" they asked slowly.

As she lowered her throwing arm, all Adelia could think to say in reply was, "What are *you* doing?"

"Breaking camp," Hero said. "I . . . I assumed that you were saddling up Zahra and Stasia, right? I thought that if I packed for both of us, we could head out sooner, maybe make it to Larto by nightfall." Their eyes were on

Adelia's knife, which was still unsheathed. "Would you mind putting that away? You're making me kind of nervous here." They lifted one hand toward their belly in an abrupt, abortive movement, and Adelia was sure that they were remembering the last time they'd watched her throw a knife in their direction.

Adelia sheathed the knife without taking her eyes off Hero. "You're—you said *we* as if—are you coming with me?" She felt very small, asking that. She didn't know how to do this. She didn't know how to be a person who would ask that question.

"Yes," Hero replied levelly, and Adelia respected that they hadn't said "of course" or something equally dishonest. "I was going to leave. I was actually . . . even before this all happened, I was going to tell you that it was time for me to go."

"I know," Adelia said.

Hero rubbed the back of their neck and appeared to find something important to study in the treeline. "But you were right, before. When you said that I tried to stop those men. I tried. But I failed. I didn't keep them from taking Ysabel. And it wouldn't be right for me to leave you on your own to get her back. Where I'm from, we . . . we don't leave people alone like that." They looked at Adelia, clenching their jaw. Their voice went stern. "I'll help you find her. And then I'm gone, understand? We get Ysabel back, and then that's the end of the line."

They didn't say more, and Adelia didn't press them. But as she led Stasia back to the pond to be saddled, she found herself swallowing around a peach pit of unspeakable words that had appeared in her throat. She pressed her face to Stasia's flank and breathed in the hippo's musty clay-smell, and gave herself permission to be relieved. She'd be alone again soon—Hero was leaving her. But not yet. Not while her baby was missing.

This, at least, she would not have to face alone.

Chapter 4

HOUNDSTOOTH STARED DOWN AT his map, twirling his grease pencil between two fingers. His left hand was smudged with black, and he was sure that he had similar marks on his face. Even as he thought it, he reached up with his smeary hand and rubbed his forehead.

"Damn it," he muttered, "where are you, Hero?"

"Houndstooth?" Archie's contralto fluted through the trees. He looked up—he didn't think he'd been gone long enough yet for her to notice and come looking for him. She'd been watching him like a hawk all day, and now—just when he'd been getting somewhere, she was interrupting him again.

His mouth twisted into a grimace as Archie's voice reached him once more. "Houndstooth! Dinner is ready. Come eat it before I give your share to Ruby!"

"Dinner?" Houndstooth looked around, blinking. Surely it wasn't time for dinner yet—he'd only told Archie that he needed to stretch his legs a few minutes after breakfast. He would surely be hungry if he'd missed lunch—but, no. The thought of food only made his stomach clench.

But the shadows were long. The day was gone—slipped right through his fingers. Houndstooth's hands turned to fists in his lap as he realized that meant another day had passed without finding Hero.

His legs ached and tingled painfully as he stood up and stretched. He'd been hunched over his maps for—well, for however long it had been. Hours, evidently. Archie would be worried—she'd try to convince him to eat and sleep and bathe, as if those things mattered when Hero was missing. As if they hadn't already wasted enough time.

Walking back through the trees, Houndstooth allowed himself to think for just an instant the thought he'd been fighting to keep at bay: *Archie is slowing you down.* He knew it wasn't true—knew that Archie was probably the only thing keeping him alive—but some small sinister part of him insisted on bringing up the idea of leaving Archie behind to focus on finding Hero.

As always, he pushed the thought away as soon as it arose—but this time, it didn't leave him easily. It was insistent: *Archie is in the way. She's a distraction.*

Houndstooth pushed his hands through his hair as he reached the sandbar where they'd made camp. It sloped down into a long, shallow bank of clear, ankle-deep water. The deeper waters that Houndstooth's inky Ruby and Archie's bone-white Rosa preferred were less than a quarter mile away, flush with the water hyacinth the hippos adored. Even now, Houndstooth could hear Ruby's pleased grunting as she grazed. He'd be fishing purple flower petals from between her teeth for days.

Archie sat on a long, weathered log that stuck out over the water on one end. It was a huge fallen tree, complete with a tangle of roots that propped it up above the water. Tadpoles and tiny fish hid in the shadows of the old, dead roots in the water, and Houndstooth couldn't help smiling at them. Between the little fish and the pristine water hyacinth, he and Archie both knew that they'd found an oasis: this place was untouched by the ravenous, terrifying scourge of the ferals.

"There you are," Archie said with a too-bright smile. "I've been thinking about where we should go next. Are you 'ungry?" She was an excellent con artist—a liar for a living—and yet when she looked at Houndstooth, she failed to conceal the worry in her eyes. Houndstooth wondered if it was because he knew her so well that he could see the lie behind her smile, or if that was simply an indicator of the depth of her concern.

Distraction, the little voice in the back of his mind whispered. *How long has it been since you've looked at the map?*

He pushed the thought away and sat next to Archie. “Here I am,” he said, trying to match her smile. He thought he did a good job, but Archie’s smile faltered as she looked at him. She handed him a tin cup full of campfire-hot stew—dried beans and hippo-belly jerky, a raft of fat and starch and salt—and a hunk of crusty bread. He made appreciative noises as he forced himself to eat. It was a good stew, he could tell that much just from looking at it, but he could barely taste it. Still, he exclaimed when he found a little fish in the bottom of his cup, cooked through, flaky and tender but small enough to eat whole. He glanced at Archie as an actor glances past the footlights, wondering if his performance was being received well.

She wasn’t even looking at him.

Archie was staring into the water, watching the little fish that darted in and out of the tree roots.

“I suppose the water here is shallow enough to keep them safe from bigger fish,” Houndstooth ventured. Archie made a noncommittal noise and stirred her stew halfheartedly. Houndstooth watched the fish alongside her in a comfortable—if odd—silence. The two of them had spent many evenings in each other’s company over the years, on one job or another, and silence between the two of them was rare at best. Both of them were natural storytellers, and whenever their conversations grew dull or seemed to be petering out, Archie would break into bawdy songs about French girls and their various flexibilities. But Houndstooth realized as he watched the fish that Archie hadn't sung once since they'd left the Harriet. In fact—he thought back over the last two months of traveling alongside his old friend—she had been silent much of the time. He hadn't noticed, since he'd been busy poring over maps and plotting routes and writing letters to contacts throughout the bayous, but Archie had been keeping her counsel. Unless, that is, she was imploring him to take better care of himself.

Houndstooth chewed on this particularly stringy bit of guilt. Something was bothering his friend, and he'd been so busy trying to avoid her care that he hadn't noticed until just now. And even now, he'd only noticed because she suddenly *wasn't* trying to take care of him.

"Are you alright, Archie?" he said after a moment's hesitation. The little voice in his head murmured that there was no time for this kind of distraction.

"Hm?" She didn't look away from the fish. "I'm fine. I'm just—fine." Houndstooth's brow creased. She'd stopped herself from saying something. It wasn't like her. Something was wrong, but—*let it go,* the little voice hissed. *Get back to the maps. Hero could be dying right now.*

"Alright," Houndstooth said, pushing away the guilt that nagged at him again. "Well, thank you for making supper. Delightful, as always." He took his cup to the water and rinsed it, then stood and watched for a few seconds as the little fish darted out from the tree roots to gulp down the fragments of bean and gristle that floated near the shore. *Aha,* Houndstooth thought. *Maybe—if I can draw Adelia out from wherever she's hiding, then I can make her tell me where Hero is*—he stopped himself from thinking *if Hero's still alive,* because there was no other option. Hero had to be alive.

They had to be.

He started to wander toward his bedroll and lantern, knowing that he would need some light. Night was falling fast, and he couldn't afford to wait. But what kind of trap should he set? Something to do with Cal, maybe? Or, no—Adelia already knew that Cal was dead, he kept forgetting. Something to do with the baby? What about—

"I think we should go to Baton Rouge," Archie said behind him.

Houndstooth turned around, cocking his head. Baton Rouge was at least three days' hard riding away, and it was practically dry. "Why on earth would you want to go there?" he asked.

Archie was looking at him with grim determination. "I think we need to regroup. I think that we should board Ruby and Rosa for a week or two while you rest and eat. And"—her eyes flicked away from his for an instant, just an instant—"I will be able to send a letter there, to Carter. I will be able to tell him where to find us. If we stayed put for a change—"

Distractions. Houndstooth trembled with sudden fury. He felt his lip twist into a sneer and before he could stop himself, he was laughing. It was not a kind laugh, and Archie flinched at the sound of it. "I see," he said in a low, smooth voice. "Of course—I should have realized that you were *pining*."

Archie's brows shot up, then drew down in confusion and hurt. Her accent was thick with shock. "Now, see 'ere, 'Oundstooth—"

"No, no, please, Archie, I insist," Houndstooth said, and even to his own ears his voice sounded cold and sharp. It was practically his father's voice. "You're absolutely right. We simply *must* spend the last of our money to board Ruby *and* Rosa *and* Abigail, so that we can go spend another two weeks wasting time while you write love letters to someone who doesn't even want you badly enough to come meet you where you are. Or do you think he'll come all the way to Baton Rouge to spend a night in your *company*?"

Archie's face darkened. She took three slow, deliberate steps toward Houndstooth. "I think," she said quietly, "you should take a walk, oui? Clear your head for a few minutes. You are not thinking straight, 'Oundstooth, my old friend."

"I'm not?" he spat. "I'm not thinking straight? Au contraire, *Regina*." Archie shook her head at him warningly, but even as he knew that he should stop he continued. "I'm the only one of us who's been thinking straight this whole time. I'm the one who's been focused on finding Hero and Adelia, while *you've* been getting distracted by—what?" He walked to her bedroll and flipped up her rough blanket with one foot, revealing a packet of letters bound with a dark green ribbon. "Love notes?" He kicked at the packet of letters, knocking it into the dirt. "Fantasies? Of a future with a *U.S. marshal*?" He kicked at the letters again furiously. His feet felt almost numb. "What, are you going to settle down with Carter, *Regina*? Are you going to have a parlor where you host fine ladies for tea and discuss the weather? Are you going to birth a litter of brats and spend your time chasing them away from the fine china? Are you going to tell stories about the days when you *used* to be a legendary hopper who was worth a *damn* to her crew, who had an ounce of loyalty, who was planning to make something of herself? Is that the life you want?" He wheeled around and pointed a shaking finger at the water. "Then go! Go get your *beau*, if you really think he'll have you."

Archie was standing very still. She was staring,

Houndstooth realized, at his feet. He looked down and saw that his left boot heel was crushing one end of the packet of letters. The green ribbon had come partially undone, and was dusky with dirt. Houndstooth wiped his mouth with the heel of his hand, feeling oddly empty and almost drunk. He swayed on his feet, once, then steadied himself.

Archie walked over to him and put her hand on his arm. She pressed it down until it rested by his side, then raised her hand to his face. She brought her fingers in front of his eyes and he could see, in the dying light of the day, that they were wet.

He reached up to feel his own face. When had he begun to cry? But there, among the stubble of his patchy beard—when had he let himself grow a beard?—was wetness.

"I think you need to go for a walk, chérie," Archie said. Her voice shook, and Houndstooth could not tell from her face what emotion caused the tremor. "Do not come back until the moon is up," she added, pressing a loving hand to his wet cheek, "or I think I will kill you."

Houndstooth nodded, then stooped to pick up the packet of letters. He pressed it into Archie's hands. She stared at the space near his right ear. "Go now," she whispered. "Go see to yourself."

Houndstooth walked into the darkening trees. As the

buzz of nocturnal insects began to rise, he let himself get lost on the little islet. He let himself get lost in the dark, and he let himself cry, although he couldn't have said what exactly the tears were for any more than he could have said who it was that he had truly been shouting at back at the camp. He wandered until it was too dark to see the trees in front of him, and then he sat on the ground and put his face in his hands and wondered if he could ever find his way back.

Chapter 5

HERO DISMOUNTED AT PORT ROUGE with an aching spine and half-numb legs. A week of hard riding along the Black River, the Red River, and a series of marshes and tributaries that dodged the Mississippi had left them feeling threadbare and ready for a week's worth of sleep. Stasia, Hero's borrowed steed, had served Hero well enough, and they patted her flank, torn between gratitude for her speed and a yearning for their old friend Abigail. Nearly all of the waters they'd ridden through had been shockingly docile, a surprise for which Hero had been infinitely thankful. They'd asked a flint-eyed dockworker at Alligator Bayou about it on their way to Thompson Creek.

"Oh, hell," he'd said, chewing on a long strip of what Hero guessed to be salt cod. "It's been a strange couple of months, what with the dam collapse and all. River's fucked. Bayou's alright, for the most part—only been a couple attacks, and them just people being stupid and all." He paused to swab sweat from his brow with his forearm, an exercise in futility as far as Hero was concerned.

"When you say 'people being stupid' . . . ?" Hero was

deeply skeptical that the ferals hadn't been an issue.

"Just don't go out at night, and watch for wakes 'thout a boat attached to 'em, and I'm sure you know the rest." He appraised Zahra and Stasia, eyeing the scars that marred the hippos' flanks, but before he could ask about where Hero and Adelia were riding from—or where they were headed—they were already gone, riding toward Port Rouge.

Port Rouge was a puddle of a marsh tucked into an elbow of the Mississippi near the top of Baton Rouge proper. It was man-made and clumsy the way most hopper wallows were—wood and stone and sandbags from a generation before walled off the shallow half mile of brown water to form a wet pit for hippos to wade in. But there was vegetation growing there, and waterbirds, and a high enough divide keeping the river out, so Hero and Adelia paid the fee to board Zahra and Stasia there with only a cursory amount of grumbling over the cost.

"Will they be alright in there?" Hero asked, looking over their shoulder as Zahra and Stasia waded over to investigate a heron.

"They'll be fine," Adelia replied distractedly as she adjusted her shirt.

"Do you really buy that the ferals are laying low?"

"I'd wager—*hnf*." Adelia adjusted her shirt again, wincing. "I'd wager that they've mostly been causing troubles farther south. That's the way the river flows, sí?"

"Still," Hero started to say.

"Still, sure, fine. Hop-blighted *damn,* this hurts." Adelia made a little pained growling noise, then abruptly stepped off the road into the thin brush beside the river.

Hero felt inexpressibly awkward. They didn't say anything, but they turned away so that Adelia could do whatever it was that she did when her breasts hurt. They tried to ignore the steady stream of curses in both English and Spanish that drifted to them from the brush, and wished that they'd known some solution to her pain. That was their whole job, and they knew it—on every team they'd ever worked with, they'd been the one who people would turn to when every idea had proven to be a bust. But this was a whole different swamp to navigate, and the best they could offer Adelia was a useless, sympathetic wince every time her swearing started to heat up. Their brain spun, trying to think of something, anything—a device, or a chemical—but they were at a total loss.

When Adelia emerged from the brush, Hero clapped their hands to their mouth to stop themselves from laughing or asking questions. The entire front of Adelia's shirt was soaked—no, Hero realized. Adelia's *entire* shirt. And her hair. It looked as though she'd dunked herself into the river.

Adelia glowered. "I spilled," she said tersely.

"Okay," Hero said—but they couldn't help themselves. "Did you jump into the water to get it back?"

Adelia started to stalk ahead, but then, to Hero's shock, she stopped and waited for them. When they caught up to her, she muttered, "I'm hot. The water makes me feel better."

Hero glanced sidelong at Adelia. Twin flags of pink rode high on her cheeks, and they allowed themselves a small smile at the notion that Adelia—stone-faced, ice-cold Adelia—might be a little embarrassed.

~

They reached Baton Rouge just before nightfall. Adelia kicked open the swinging doors of the Hop's Tusk with one booted foot. Her hair and shirt were dry, but she'd been swearing a steady blue streak for the past hour, and Hero pitied the poor soul that got between her and her bedroom. Sure enough, Adelia stormed the bar and slapped money down on the scarred wood with a flat palm. Hero slipped into the shadows beside the door and watched as the garter-armed innkeeper behind the bar handed Adelia a key and snatched his hand back as though he were afraid to lose it. Adelia made for the stairs, pushing her way through the crowd with a stiff shoulder, and then she was gone.

Hero eased their way to the bar and sat, groaning at the relief their legs felt. They doubted that they'd be able to get up again any time soon, and debated asking the innkeeper for a pillow, a blanket, and twenty-four hours to sit on the stool without moving.

They scrubbed their face with their hands, trying not to let their eyes close for too long. When they lowered their hands, there was a drink sweating on the bar in front of them.

"Excuse me?" they called, and the innkeeper slid over to them. He was a sallow-faced white man with drooping, hound-dog eyes and a few fine wisps of hair stretched across a freckled scalp. Hero reflected that the poor wilted fellow looked like he'd rather have been on a burning raft in the middle of a lake of hippo shit than standing behind that bar. His eyes darted continuously along the nearly empty stretch of the bar, watching for someone else who might possibly need his attention.

"Yes?" he said, still not looking directly at Hero. "Is there a problem?"

"I didn't order this drink," Hero said.

The innkeeper unfolded a handkerchief and dabbed sweat from his top lip. "It's on the house. Courtesy of, hm. The lady." Hero thought for a mad instant that he meant Adelia, but then he gestured at a woman who was perched at the far end of the bar, nursing her own drink.

She didn't look up, and Hero quickly looked away, their face and neck burning in a rising flush.

They couldn't remember the last time that someone had sent them a drink at a bar. They couldn't remember the last time they'd *been* in a bar without being on a job.

The drink looked very good. But . . . *Houndstooth.*

Hero took a deep breath. *Don't think about it.* They grabbed their drink and took a long, deep slug of the brown liquor. It went down oily and hot, and burned in their belly like a live coal. They tried to pay attention to the heat, to the vile taste of the alcohol. They didn't admit to themself that they were hoping it would scald away the thought of what had happened on the Harriet after they'd left.

Hero took another drink, even though it made their eyes water. They wondered if that was what other people thought poison was like going down. So undeniable. They traced a finger through the ring of condensation on the wood in front of them, smudging it into a long oval. Remembering when a long, slim finger had traced that oval onto the inky hide of a hippo named Ruby.

They finished the drink too fast and their head was swimming. But it was better than thinking about other people swimming. Or failing to swim.

All the papers, all the songs, all the stories. They had all said the same thing: *no survivors.* And now all the booze was gone, and Hero felt a crack forming in the dam that held back all the things they had been trying not to think about.

"Well, that's one way to tell a gal you'd like her company."

Hero jumped, looked at the stool next to them. The woman—no, Hero corrected themself, the *girl,* for she couldn't have been older than seventeen or eighteen—the *girl* from the end of the bar had settled herself next to Hero. Her dark hair was barely longer than a razor would allow, and her warm brown skin was just a few shades lighter than Hero's own. She looked almost familiar, but something about the way she carried herself told Hero that it was probably this girl's job to look familiar.

Hero coughed. "Sorry, I—uh. I sort of—I'm tired," they finished weakly. "It's been a long day."

"A long week, I should think," the girl said, taking a sip of her drink. Hero did a double-take, and the girl laughed. She flagged down the innkeeper and signaled for another round before Hero could stop her.

"How did—who are you?" Hero asked, suddenly acutely aware that they were alone. Adelia, with all her weaponry and her sure aim and her expertise, was gone. They were on their own, and if this girl turned out to be trouble . . . they would have to do a better job of defending themself than they had back on the Catahoula.

"Call me Acadia," the girl drawled. "It's not my real name, but you don't need to know that and I'm not going to tell it to you. Thanks, handsome," she said, tipping a wink at the innkeeper as he dropped off two more drinks. He looked at Hero, and his eyes seemed to flash a warning. *Too late,* Hero thought, and raised their glass to Acadia.

"Are you going to kill me?" Hero asked, their throat tight. It wasn't as hard to ask as they'd thought it would be. Out of habit, they slid their free hand into their pocket. A vial of powder was there, always at the ready. One puff of air across the cork would blow more than enough of the poison into this "Acadia's" eyes. She'd be foaming from every orifice within seconds, dead within minutes. Hero let their thumbnail sink into the wax seal around the cork, but not all the way. Not yet.

Acadia glanced at them out of the corner of her eye. She didn't laugh, a small mercy for which Hero was profoundly thankful. "Not tonight," she said mildly. "Maybe another time, if you need killing."

"Well. Alright," Hero said, slipping their hand back out of their pocket, leaving the tiny vial unopened. It was a reasonable enough answer, all things considered. They sipped at the drink the innkeeper had brought, knowing that they'd end up drunk if they kept it up, but not able to will themself to care. "What can I do for you, then, *Acadia*?"

"I think we're from the same place, you and I," Acadia said. "Your accent is a little faded, but I can hear it."

Hero cocked a half smile at the girl. "I don't think we are, but that's a very nice try."

Acadia shrugged. "I would swear I've seen you before."

"Maybe on a wanted poster," Hero muttered into their glass.

"You gave up that life a long time ago, though," the girl said, and again Hero found themself staring at her, incredulous. "Oh, I know all about you, Hero Shackleby. You had quite a storied career. Although I've always wondered—I mean, everyone wonders—"

"What do you want?" Hero snapped. They didn't have the time or the energy to dance that old, familiar dance. The whelp was going to ask Hero why they'd retired, it was as obvious as a hop's hunger for milk, and Hero just . . . couldn't have that conversation. Not now.

The girl put her palms up in surrender. "Okay, alright, I'm sorry." She poked Hero in the shoulder with a nail-bitten finger. "Sensitive. The drinks were supposed to ease you up a little, you know."

Hero snorted into their glass.

"Well, fine. I've got something I'm supposed to give you." She pulled a limp piece of paper out from between her breasts. She laid it on the bar between them and added, "But I'd appreciate if you didn't read it until I was gone."

"Who's it from?"

"Read it and find out."

"That's fair," Hero said. If the girl was a messenger, she'd just finished doing her duty. Hero could respect that. Messengers weren't paid enough to keep information on their employers a secret, but they also weren't paid enough to get tangled up in the interpersonal dramas that trailed between people they didn't know.

The girl sipped her drink again, and Hero noticed that she was barely swallowing any of it. *Clever.* "So," she asked, her voice a shade too casual. "Is it true that you're here with Adelia Reyes?"

Hero didn't answer.

"I'm sure you don't want to tell me," the girl continued. "It's just that, I've been wanting to meet her ever since I was a little girl."

Hero snorted again. "You're still a little girl," they said.

The girl's eyes flashed. "I've killed men," she said in a low voice. "I think that qualifies me for something more than 'little girl.'"

"We've all killed men," Hero said—but then they gentled their voice and tried to remember a time when having killed a man had meant something significant to them, too. "I'm sure Adelia'd love to meet you." The girl rolled her eyes at the polite lie. "Or . . . she'd find it acceptable, at least. Are you staying here?"

The girl shook her head. "When she wants to meet me, just have her tell the innkeeper. He'll make sure I get the message." She looked at Hero with an entrepreneurial gleam in her eye. "And, hey. If you ever need anyone for a job, you know how to find me. My fees are very reasonable."

"So you don't work for my secret admirer?" Hero said, waving the note.

"I don't work for anybody," Acadia drawled. "I work for money. If you've got some you're looking to offload, you just let me know. Don't forget what I said about Adelia, either."

Hero took a last long drink from their glass, swallowing hard. They could feel the liquor winding its way around their arms and legs and throat, pulling them down toward drunken sleep. It was a delicious sensation.

"I'll tell her," they started to say. But they heard the swinging doors at the front of the inn creak and thump open, and by the time they looked up, Acadia already had one foot out the door.

~

"Adelia?" Hero rapped one knuckle hard on the warped

wood of the door at the end of the upstairs hallway.

"Momento," Adelia called from inside. Hero leaned against the cracked plaster wall to wait until Adelia was done with whatever ministrations her swollen breasts still required. They nudged the straw and sawdust that littered the floor with their foot, sweeping a clean arc of wood planks.

Don't think about it, they told themself, firmly shoving aside the memory of the last time they'd shared accommodations with someone. *Not now.*

"Okay, come in," Adelia said behind them. She'd opened the door and walked away, leaving Hero standing in the open doorway with their hands in their pockets. One hand crushed the already rumpled note from Acadia. Or, from whoever Acadia worked for.

Adelia leaned out of the sole window, emptying a small washbasin into the alley below. A smell filled the small room—buttermilk and sweat and earth, suspended in the humidity of the night. Adelia's thin linen shirt, unencumbered by her usual leather engirdment of sheaths, stuck to her back, and her loosely tied hair had sprung into damp curls around her face and at the nape of her neck. A flush colored the back of her neck, and Hero frowned.

It wasn't that warm in the room.

It was warm, sure, and humid as a hop's armpit, but it

was no worse than it had been during their long ride. And they couldn't ever remember seeing Adelia sweat before.

"Are you alright?" they asked, unthinking. They flinched—Adelia wasn't the kind of person who liked to be worried about.

"I'm fine," Adelia snapped. "Why?"

She turned and Hero's frown deepened. Two bright, high spots of color had risen in her cheeks, and her eyes were bright.

"Do you have a fever, Adelia?" Hero stepped forward, putting their hand out to feel Adelia's forehead before they had time to think better of it. There was a flash of movement, a shout—and then Hero was on the floor, their face pressed into unfresh sawdust and grime, their arm twisted painfully high behind their back above an acute weight that they could only assume was—yes, it had to be a knee pressing into their spine.

A moment later, the weight was gone, and their arm was free. They scrambled up and saw Adelia standing a few feet away, one hand pressed to her forehead.

"Oh, Hero—I'm, hm." She cleared her throat awkwardly. "I'm sorry. I didn't—I didn't mean to, ah. To . . ."

"To flatten me?" Hero asked wryly, rolling their shoulder until it popped.

"I don't like to be touched without permission," Adelia said in a quiet voice that carried what Hero thought to be a shadow of regret. "I'm very sorry."

"It's alright," Hero said. "I should have asked. Can we call it even?"

Adelia nodded, then looked awkwardly away. The tension of unfulfilled violence hung in the air, and Hero wondered what would have happened if Adelia's weapons hadn't been safely stowed by the time they came in. They were willing to bet that there would be blood on the floor of the little bedroom.

Best to not think about that, either, they told themself, even as their hand drifted up to the scar on their belly.

"Well," Hero said in an overjovial voice, forcing themself to sound calm. "At any rate. I have something you should see."

Adelia raised her eyebrows. "Oh?"

"Here," Hero said. They pulled the folded paper out of their hip pocket, unfolding it before they handed it over. "A message."

"From who?" Adelia demanded, eyes flashing.

"The one and only; Whelan Parrish," Hero answered. "Via a girl named Acadia. Does the name ring a bell?"

"No," Adelia said absently as she scanned the note. "Should it?"

"I don't think so," Hero said. "But she'd like it to."

"Maldito." Adelia tugged at her shirt, fanning herself. "This is—me cago en la madre que te parió! We have to go. Parrish—we have to go and meet him—"

Hero held up a hand and sat hard on the bed. "Not tonight."

"Not tonight?" Adelia's chin snapped up and she glared at Hero with a ferocity that made Hero long for the ferals on the Harriet. "*Not tonight*?! I'm sorry, Hero, did you have somewhere else to be? This man has *Ysabel* and he's probably going to—"

"Here," Hero said simply. "I have to be *here*. And so do you, Adelia. We need to rest. We need to bathe. We need to regroup. He isn't going to hurt the baby tonight, but if we go see him and try to take her back in the state we're in right now? We'll both wind up dead, and then there'll be no one left to kill the sorry son of a bitch." *And besides,* they didn't say, *you're not thinking straight, you fever-brained loon.*

Adelia fumed for a moment, but Hero knew that she'd see the truth in what they had said.

"Fine," she finally snapped. "But we go first thing in the morning, after we eat and . . . and wash, and make a plan. Dawn. We leave at dawn."

"That sounds perfect," Hero said. "Now, how about some sleep?" They tried out a smile, but Adelia just snarled at them. They shrugged mildly, then leaned back against the headboard and lowered their hat over their eyes.

Adelia would sleep eventually. If those fever flags flying on her cheeks were any indication, she'd probably sleep even better than Hero intended to. She'd have to, or else they'd need to wait another day before going to find Ysabel.

It'll be fine, Hero thought, peeking out from under their hat at Adelia's pacing, watching her eyes glitter with rage and fever and murder. *She can wait. Vengeance is a slow game.*

Hero had always been good at slow games.

Chapter 6

THE RIDE TO BATON ROUGE had been a silent one. The intervening week, on the other hand, hadn't been silent—it had been something much worse.

It had been polite.

"I will be back in an hour," Archie said, settling a brushed felt bowler over her slicked-back hair. She'd borrowed Houndstooth's straight razor to hone her crisp part; her hair looked better than his had in months. "Please do not feel the need to wait for me to 'ave supper."

Houndstooth didn't look up from the letter he was writing. "Thank you for letting me know."

Archie pursed her lips for a moment, then shot her cuffs and walked out the door without another word. The tension between her and Houndstooth had been thick as hop fat for the past eight days, and she didn't know how to cut through it. They'd fought before, more than enough times—but never like this.

She walked down out of the townhouse where she and Houndstooth were staying and onto the street. Her gold-tipped cane flashed in the late-morning sun, and she felt a weight slip from her shoulders as she brushed the brim of her hat at two young ladies, who giggled back from under their shared parasol.

Not her type, but it was nice to see them blush.

She knew she was handsome. Her pinstriped linen suit was painful to keep free of wrinkles while she was traveling, but it fit her like a dream and was better tailored than the suits of most of the men she tipped her hat to on the street. The last time she'd worn it, she'd been riding through the night to get her hands on enough explosives to ruin a dam.

She preferred the way the fabric looked in the sunlight.

Oh yes—she knew she was handsome. Even Houndstooth's eyes had flashed with envy the first time he saw her waistcoat—dove-grey paisley with the slightest sheen of lilac. She smiled to herself, remembering how she'd salted the wound by telling him that her Parisian tailor would only accept clients in person. She always enjoyed dressing herself more when she could share her flashes of sartorial brilliance with her friend.

"Pardonnez-moi, sir?" Archie looked down to find a hunched girl tugging at her coattail. The girl was young, too thin, and had grease smeared across the dark brown skin of her face. She smiled tentatively up at Archie. "Sir, could you spare a coin for a poor, hungry girl?"

"For you, girl?" Archie reached into her coat as though

she were pulling out a pocketbook. "Of course I could spare a coin. Although not if you're going to *steal* it from me." She pulled a slim Châtellerault blade from the inside pocket of her jacket, flicking it open under the girl's chin. Her other hand gripped the girl's wrist as she pulled the girl's hand from the pocket of her vest. Her watch dangled from between the girl's fingers.

The girl's face split into a wide grin. "Damn," she whispered, careful not to bump her jaw against Archie's knife. "I should have gone for the knife instead of the watch."

"Oui, so you should 'ave," Archie agreed. "The mother-of-pearl on the grip would've kept you fed for a week. That is, if I didn't find you first, and slit your belly open like a lake trout."

Keeping a grip on the girl's wrist so her pocket watch couldn't vanish, Archie ducked into one of the narrow alleys that scored the street. She extracted her watch from the girl's grip and tucked it into her interior jacket pocket, along with the closed knife. The girl withdrew a handkerchief from her blouse and wiped the grease from her face with an effort.

"You should smudge it more around your mouth," Archie advised. "When you just do the cheekbones and the jaw, it makes you look too pretty to be an urchin. And per'aps grow out your hair? This fuzz," she said, gesturing to the too-short-to-curl cut, "it is very recognizable in this city."

The girl pursed her lips. "Thanks," she muttered, looking put out.

"You're welcome for the free advice," Archie said dryly, tugging her waistcoat straight. "You'll 'ave your coin if you've brought me news." The girl's eyes flicked toward the mouth of the alley, and Archie clicked her tongue. "Do not play games with me, Acadia. Have you seen him, or no?"

"No," Acadia finally admitted.

"You're sure?" Archie deflated a little, resisting the urge to lean against the wall of the alley. Despair or no, that grime wouldn't scrub out of her linen pinstripes easily.

"I'm sure," Acadia said tartly. "I would know if I'd seen a six-foot-four black man wearing a marshal's star around here. You're not the only person who would pay for that kind of information, you know."

Archie sighed. "Fine. I'll see you tomorrow, oui? I'll come downtown around . . . noon, I think. It will be my last day 'ere—even if you don't see 'im, you'll 'ave coin for your trouble."

Acadia seemed to soften. "Hey, he'll show up," she said. "I know for sure that your letters posted—I gave them to my best rider. I'm sure he'll be here." She patted Archie's arm awkwardly, then gave the collar of her jacket a tug. "And if you keep dressing up this nice, you'll look damned fine when you meet him."

She winked and turned on her heel, walking out of the alley and leaving Archie behind. Archie took a deep breath, telling herself that the girl was right. Carter would show up.

He always did. Even if it took a year. He always showed up.

Archie straightened her jacket where Acadia had tugged it out of line. She reached into the breast pocket for her watch to check the time as she walked out of the alley, then swore. She looked up and down the street, whipping her bowler off in frustration—but there was no sign of the girl who had just stolen both her pocket watch *and* her Châtellerault.

~

By the time Archie got back to the townhouse, Houndstooth was gone. She breathed a sigh of relief as she walked in and shucked off her jacket, which was clinging to her arms despite the light weight of the fabric. She had been hoping to talk to him about the next part of their journey—but she'd also been dreading it.

She walked into the dining room, of a mind to investigate any breakfast leftovers Houndstooth had abandoned. If there were any good pastries left over, she would go and visit Rosa down at Port Rouge. She'd been there at least every other day. She didn't like boarding Rosa—the albino hippo's skin inevitably dried out at the neglectful hands of the half-drunk hoppers who ran the port. A pastry now and then felt like the very least she could do.

When she opened the French doors to the dining room, all thoughts of Rosa fled her mind as she stifled a scream.

The white jacquard wallpaper was marred with wicked holes and slashes. Letters were pinned to the wall with a collection of tiny throwing knives. Phrases and words in the letters were circled with grease pencil; some of the letters had thick, smudgy black lines drawn between them, stretching across paper and wallpaper alike. Question marks, crosses, and overlapping circles were drawn at irregular intervals.

In the center of the wall, Houndstooth's map hung askew like a head on a pike. A fat oval was drawn around Baton Rouge.

"'E's lost 'is mind," Archie breathed, staring at the ruined wall. She swore under her breath; then, dissatisfied, she swore over her breath. She threw her jacket onto the table as she stalked across the room to stare at the wall.

They were letters, she realized, from all of Houndstooth's contacts across the country. There were letters from old enemies in New York, people whose names he couldn't say without spitting. There was a letter from the lover who had abandoned him. There were letters from people he'd worked with and people he'd swindled and people who had left tooth marks on his fists.

He'd circled key phrases in each—"I haven't even heard of that person" was circled in one letter, with the word "LIE" scribbled above it. "Near Houston" was circled in another, with "HERO WOULD NEVER" scrawled across the words. The map was covered with notes and references to letters and dates, with arrows pointing to cities.

But Baton Rouge was the place he'd circled. And now he was gone.

Archie swore again. A really good swear—a streak that would have curled the hair on Cal Hotchkiss' toes, the devil rest him. How had she failed to notice? How had he carried out all of this correspondence right under her nose? She thought back to her nights out avoiding him, her trips to rendezvous with her own messengers—and she realized that it had probably been child's play for Houndstooth to work around her all this time.

Then she rolled up her sleeves and started removing letters from the wall, laying them out on the dining room table. Once she'd re-created Houndstooth's tableau, she hitched up her pants and sat in one of the plush, high-backed chairs that circled the table.

She picked up the nub of grease pencil that Houndstooth had left behind, and then she got to work trying to figure out where it was that he had gone.

~

Six hours later, Archie was slapping open the swinging wooden doors of the Hop's Tusk with both hands. She stood in the doorway, letting her eyes adjust to the low light inside the bar. The heat of the gaslamp just outside the doors warmed her back. She tilted back the brim of her bowler and used her cane to hold the door open beside her.

She saw him at the bar before her eyes finished adjusting. His hat was on the stool next to him, and he was slumped over the scarred wood of the bar, his eyes fixed on a glass of brown liquor.

Archie sat next to him, picking up his hat. She tugged the bottom of her vest down more sharply than was strictly necessary to make the fabric lie smooth. She tried to decide whether she should kill Houndstooth. She tried to decide if it would be a mercy to do so.

"I'm not drunk," he said after a long time.

"Fine," Archie replied. She could hear how taut her voice was, and tried to take a slow, deep breath.

"I've been staring at this same damned glass for three hours," he said. "Waiting."

"For me?" Archie said, knowing that wasn't the answer.

"For them," he whispered. He looked up at Archie, and fervor burned in his eyes. "They're here, Archie. Both of them. Hero and Adelia—they're *here,* I know it."

"Chérie—"

"No, Archie, *no*!" He shook his head hard. "They're *here,* they're *staying here,* and I'm going to find them and I'm going to *find Hero* and—"

"I don't think they're 'ere," Archie murmured. "You misunderstood, 'Oundstooth. I think Hero is dead."

Houndstooth shot up from his stool, and before Archie's eyes could track the movement he was holding a knife to her cheek.

"Don't you dare—" He nudged his cheek with a rolled-up sleeve, his eyes fierce and glassy. "Don't you say that. They're not dead. I would know."

"If they're not dead," Archie said softly, feeling the burn of Houndstooth's blade as it scored her cheek, "why haven't they written to you?"

Houndstooth's arm drifted down, then snapped back up. "Adelia probably isn't letting them," he said.

"Why would Adelia keep them alive?" Archie asked, and Houndstooth's lips pursed. He swallowed hard around his total lack of an answer.

His eyes slid away from hers. Archie eased the knife from his hand too easily. She laid a hand on his shoulder and pressed down until he was slumped on his barstool again.

"They can't be dead," he said to the glass of whiskey. "We . . . we deserve better than that. Hero deserves *better* than that."

"It might not be about 'deserves,'" Archie said. She tried to keep her voice soft, gentle. Kind. She picked up Houndstooth's glass and pressed it into his grease-smudged hand. "It's time to stop looking, mon frère. You are killing yourself."

Houndstooth looked hollow on the barstool next to her. He'd always been thin, but now Archie realized that he looked desiccated—like a crumbling leaf. He looked ready to disintegrate at a touch. Rather than test his strength, Archie pressed two fingers to the bottom of his glass and nudged it up toward his face.

He drained it, then slammed the glass down on the bar, gasping. Archie raised an arm to signal to the pinch-faced innkeeper for two more drinks. He nodded from across the bar, then continued wiping out the same glass he'd been drying since Archie walked in. He eyed them from under furrowed brows. Then, his eyes darted to the door an instant before it banged open.

"Archie!" A dark blur rushed across the bar, stopping just far enough away from Archie to avoid being grabbed. The girl was breathless, bone-thin, and swimming in layers of royal blue satin. She looked like she'd run from a dance hall ten miles away. But then the girl whipped off the hat—and the hair with it—and propped a leg on the barstool next to Archie.

"Acadia?" Archie gaped at the girl. "Where did you get that dress?"

"From the none of your goddamned business surplus store," Acadia snapped, pulling a letter out of her boot. "Here," she said, and thrust the rolled-up paper at Archie. Archie took it, and before she could unfurl it, Acadia had replaced her wig and hat and was on her way out the door, and then was turning on her heel to snatch the letter back.

"You can read it after you pay me," she said, holding out her other hand.

"And will you be returning my watch in exchange? And my knife?" Archie held out a hand, and after her Châtellerault and timepiece had been deposited into it, pulled out a billfold from her breast pocket. She traded the girl more than she'd agreed to pay in order to get the letter back, more than the letter should have been worth. As she started to unroll it again, Acadia disappeared through the swinging doors, running as fast as her feet would carry her.

Archie read the letter. She read it again. And she read it halfway through again before the still-swinging doors were stilled by a large pair of calloused hands. A shadow filled the doorway. One of those hands reached up to remove a battered black leather hat with a glinting silver star on the brim.

Archie looked up as Gran Carter entered the Hop's Tusk. Behind her, Houndstooth was still staring into his empty glass—but he looked up as Carter's booming voice filled the room.

"Archie?"

Archie stared at him with wide eyes, the letter dangling from her fingers. He crossed the room in a few long strides, cupped her face in his hands, and kissed her with all the desperation of a drowning man pushing his way into a pocket of air. He knocked her bowler hat off, tangling one hand in the lapel of her waistcoat, and pressed the full length of his body to hers. She grabbed the front of his duster in two fists, crumpling his own letter against his chest—but after a long moment, she pushed him away.

"Archie," he breathed again, pressing his forehead to hers. His voice was a bonfire. "I missed you so goddamn much."

"Carter—"

"Did you get my letter?"

"Just now," she said. She squeezed her fist against his chest, and the paper crinkled against him.

"Just now? But—if you didn't read it before, then why are you here?" He looked toward the bar, where Houndstooth had braced his elbows on the counter and was holding his head in his hands.

"We didn't know," Archie started—then she corrected herself. "I didn't know."

Carter kissed Archie again, more briefly this time, and then started for the stairs. Archie followed fast on his heels, unsheathing a long, wicked length of steel from within her cane.

Houndstooth looked up at both of them, then stood from his barstool. "Where are you two going?" He stooped to pick up the paper that Archie had dropped to the floor. He scanned it, then looked up to where Carter and Archie were running up the staircase. "Hey!"

Archie paused, gripping the banister in one hand and her blade in the other. "I was wrong," she said, "you 'ad it right. 'Oundstooth"—Houndstooth was already halfway to the foot of the stairs by the time Archie finished—"they're *here*."

Chapter 7

BANG.

Adelia's fingers were slipping.

"Let go!" Hero called up. The words echoed faintly. Adelia's fingers reflexively clenched around the wood of the windowsill as another *bang* echoed from within the room. He was breaking down the door.

"Adelia," Hero hissed again, "Let go, I'll catch you! It's not that far!"

The next *bang* was accompanied by a *crunch* and then a shout. Adelia felt one of her fingernails split as she dug it into the wood of the windowsill—she flinched as a splinter slid into her nail bed, and then the world spun, and then she was falling.

"*Oof—ghhuuuuh—*" Hero was staggering under her, and then she was on her feet, although she still felt like she was falling. A firm hand on her back, and normally she would flinch away but the hand was cold even through her damp, clinging, too-hot shirt. It felt nice, like cool water—and then the cool hand was pushing her, and then they were running as shouts drifted down from the open window like blossoms falling from a magnolia tree.

A hat settled onto Adelia's head, and the cool hand was pushing her into an alley, and then Hero was beside her, breathing hard with their back pressed to wall and their face turned to the street.

"Fuck," Hero panted, wiping their forehead and throat with their kerchief. "Fuck, that was close."

"What happened?" Adelia's voice was raspy, shaking, and she realized belatedly that she was shivering. Hero noticed and shucked off their coat. As they reached across her to pull it over her shoulders, their forearm brushed her left breast, and pain erupted all through her chest. Her vision tunneled.

"Whoa, there," Hero said, catching Adelia before she could fall. "Whoa, now—"

And then Adelia was the one falling like a magnolia blossom; she watched the ground float up toward her, watched Hero's hands flutter into her field of vision, watched a hat—her hat?—land in front of her. The world slid sideways, and then she was looking at the saddlebag that rested on the ground between Hero's boots, and then she closed her eyes and slid into blessedly still darkness.

~

Adelia woke up drowning.

She sputtered, her arms spasming. She reached out and grasped at the first soft thing she found. Her fingers were weak, sore as hell from gripping the window, but she tightened her grip with a will when the subject of her grasp let out a high-pitched noise. With her other hand, she pushed her hair out of her stinging eyes, blinking away water mixed with what must have been either her own sweat or her own blood. She sat up as she did it, ignoring how the movement made her head spin.

"Let—*go*—"

Adelia blinked a few more times and a dark face came into focus, barely visible by the thin light of the clouded-over moon.

"Hero?" she asked, and then she realized with horror that her weak fingers were clutching at Hero's throat. She pulled her hand away—god, no, for the second time in a day she'd almost—

"Lo siento," she rasped, her voice hoarse. She felt as though she'd swallowed a bolt of burlap. Hero was coughing, tears streaming down their face, and Adelia felt a flush of shame fighting her urge to shiver. "Why am I wet? What happened?"

Hero was too busy gasping to answer, so Adelia looked around. She was sitting in reddish clay, in a puddle. There was an ewer knocked over next to Hero, and a puddle.

Not drowning, then. Revived.

Adelia pressed her hands to her face, ignoring the feeling of cool clay slipping between her fingers and her cheeks. She was exhausted, felt as though she'd just ridden Zahra a thousand miles overland while carrying Stasia on her shoulders. She took a deep, slow breath, and realized that she could smell her own sweat over the rich decomposition smell of clay.

A groan and a splash sounded from behind her, not close but not far either. She startled, looked—and there, nosing at the edge of the paddock, was Hero's old hippo, Abigail.

"Hero," Adelia breathed. "Hero—*Hero*!" She slapped at Hero's arm, and they glared at her, rubbing their throat.

"Yeah, welcome back to life," they snapped. "Carried your ass all the damn way here, and I don't mind telling you that you haven't hardly lost that baby weight enough for my scrawny self to—"

"*Shut up,*" Adelia said, grabbing Hero by the chin before they could flinch away. "Tell me later. *Look.*"

She directed Hero's chin, and their features clenched with the unmistakable air of patience about to reach a breaking point—but then they saw Abigail, and their face went slack.

"It can't be," Hero breathed. They scrambled up, slipping in the wet clay, and ran to the edge of the paddock.

They reached right through the half-rotted wood at the edge of the water and pressed both hands to the nose of the little Standard Grey hippo that was huffing bubbles into the water there.

"It had better be," Adelia said, "or else you just grabbed a strange hippo by the face."

But Hero didn't hear her. They were weeping, their face pressed between Abigail's nostrils. They hadn't seen her since the night the Harriet fell, the night they had nearly died, two months before—a night that suddenly felt so, so far away.

While Hero sobbed all over Abigail, Adelia rested her head in her hands and tried to piece the night together. Her thoughts were disjointed and slow, and her left breast throbbed with a steady pain, as though a hot coal had been inserted behind her nipple by someone with a steady hand and an eye for detail.

It hadn't hurt this badly when she'd expressed her milk back at the inn, while Hero was downstairs at the bar—but her breast had been hot and red, swollen-looking. *Infection,* she thought, remembering the sickly smell of the milk she'd washed out of her shirt when they'd first arrived at Port Rouge. It had hurt then, and the pain was even worse now.

She remembered going to sleep at Hero's behest.

She remembered waking up to a pounding on the

door, and the sound of Hero talking to the mousy little innkeeper. She remembered the murmured exchange, catching the words "U.S. marshal" in the instant before Hero tore the blankets from her and pulled her out of bed.

She remembered Hero urging her out the window as footsteps hammered down the hall outside their door. She remembered the sounds of the door being broken down.

So, Adelia thought. This was it. He'd found her. Gran Carter had tracked her down—and he wasn't alone.

"Hero," she said abruptly. "Hero, we need to talk."

"In a minute," Hero said.

"It's important."

Hero didn't answer. Adelia looked up and saw that they were staring across the water at a patch of reeds that swayed gently in the cool night air. They were saying something that almost sounded like "Ruby."

"Hero?" Adelia hauled herself upright and walked over to the paddock to stand next to Hero as they held up a hand for silence. Abigail huffed warm air over Adelia's fingers, then dismissed her as having nothing to offer and returned her attention to Hero, who patted her nose absently. "What is it?" Adelia asked.

"I thought I saw something," Hero murmured. Their eyes were fixed on the reeds, which had gone still. Across the water, a hippo muttered to itself or someone else, then let out a long bleating groan. Hero shook their head, then looked at Adelia. "You look better," they said. "We should ride while your fever is down. I think it broke while I was carrying you here. At least, you were sweating like it had broken." They grimaced, and Adelia gave them a sympathetic frown.

"Thank you," Adelia finally managed, feeling awkward as she said it. "For saving me."

Hero shrugged uncomfortably and began performing an unnecessarily thorough inspection of Abigail's ears. "Wasn't anything you wouldn't have done for me," they muttered, and Adelia felt tears spring to her eyes. That wasn't something anyone had ever said about her before.

"Hero," she began—but then Hero straightened, wiping their hands on their pants, and shook their head.

"We'll talk about it later," they said. "For now, we need to go. We can't stay here." They started walking toward the locked tack shed next to the paddock, and Abigail began hauling herself out of the water, following her hopper. The hippo lumbered over to Adelia, water streaming from her belly, and nosed at her shoulder.

"Hola, Abi," Adelia whispered, wiping at her eyes. She gave the hippo's shoulder a pat as Hero swore at the lock on the tack shed. They had their eyes right up next to it, straining to manipulate their lock picks by moonlight.

"Your Hero over there is something else, eh? What do you think—would you trust them?" Abigail gave no reply, but continued to drip as Adelia rubbed her side. "I thought so," Adelia murmured. "I thought you would say that."

Hero returned a few minutes later, carrying Abigail's riding saddle in their arms.

"I don't know who found her," they said, "but they've been taking good care of her. I thought this whole time that maybe—when the Harriet—" Their voice broke, and they didn't continue. After a moment, they shook their head and made a noise like they were swallowing a piece of glass. "Never mind," they muttered, and they saddled Abigail in silence.

The hippo entered the water with no great urgency, pausing frequently to flip her ears and duck her head. "No point rushing her," Hero shrugged after Adelia's third sidelong glance at them. "She likes to move at her own pace, Abigail does. Meantime, we should figure out where it is you want to go. Somewhere Carter won't be able to find us, I should think."

"Where I *want* to go is to a house in the country with a bathtub and a soft bed," Adelia said. Abigail finished blowing bubbles in the water, and presented herself at the water's edge. "Where I'm *going* to go? That should be obvious."

"Where *we're* going to go. Enlighten me," Hero drawled, swinging themself into the saddle and holding out a hand to Adelia. There was just enough room on the saddle for both of them. Adelia gripped the webbing on Abigail's harness and adjusted the grip of her thighs on the sides of the saddle.

"We're going to visit Whelan Parrish," Adelia replied. "We're going to find out what the hell it is that he wants. And then we're going to get Ysabel back."

As Abigail set off, a splash sounded from behind them. Hero, who was bent forward and cooing into Abigail's ear, didn't seem to notice. Adelia looked over her shoulder and saw that the reeds were moving again. A bone-white nose stuck up out of the water for a moment before disappearing again below the surface.

"Did you say something?" Hero asked.

"No," Adelia replied. "I thought I saw—no, never mind," she said, shaking her head. "It was nothing."

It had been nothing. A trick of the moonlight on the water. As they rode out of Port Rouge, Adelia began to shiver again. She told herself that it was just her fever, returning in earnest and making her see things. *It's only the fever,* she told herself. *Don't tell Hero about your hallucinations. You'll only reopen the wound.* Her conscience twitched. *Haven't you hurt them enough?*

~

"Adelia?"

Adelia startled awake. She couldn't remember the last time she'd woken naturally. Whether she was startling awake because the baby was crying or because someone was trying to catch her or because she was dreaming about blood and death—it didn't matter. She was always stuttering into consciousness, her breath in her throat and her heart pounding.

"What is—what?" she said, her voice rasping in her throat. Her mouth tasted like a dead thing. A canteen appeared before her, and she drained it before she could think to turn it away. *You're getting complacent,* she scolded herself.

"Thought you might want to wake up," Hero said mildly over their shoulder. "We're getting into an iffy part of the water."

Adelia blinked, took in her surroundings. It was bright out, startlingly bright, and the air over the surface of the water teemed with dragonflies. Abigail was pushing forward through a thicket of water hyacinth quickly enough that Adelia guessed the hippo had eaten her fill a ways back. But she could see what Hero was worried about: a few hundred feet ahead of them, the hyacinth started to thin, exposing the muddy waters of Thompson Creek.

"I'm awake," Adelia said, and she reached instinctively for a weapon, any weapon. Her throwing knives were still strapped to her left arm, and the long, curved knife she kept strapped to her thigh was still there—but the rest of her weapons, she realized belatedly, were still back at the Hop's Tusk.

Adelia suddenly felt very naked.

"Don't be too nervous," Hero said. "I don't think any ferals will have made it this far up the creek. And if they did, they've probably been gorging themselves on whatever was living in here. So they shouldn't be too hungry, I don't think."

"I'm not nervous," Adelia snapped, scanning the surface of the water. It was still, save for the water bugs that skimmed back and forth, waiting to be eaten by enterprising fish.

"Sure," Hero said. "Anyway, I'd say we're just a few more hours away from the place Parrish told us to meet him. We're not making bad time at all. Wondered if you might want to talk about what it is that we're going to do when we get there?"

Adelia wanted so badly to growl that they'd kill Parrish on sight—but she knew that wouldn't be the case, and she suspected that Hero would see right through her. "I don't know," she finally admitted. "I suppose we will have to wait and see."

"He won't have Ysabel anywhere we can get to her," Hero said. "You know that, right?"

"I know," Adelia murmured, hating that Hero was right. "We will have to figure it out when we arrive. I . . ." She faltered.

"You don't want to guess," Hero filled in. "You don't want to try to make a plan that will inevitably turn out to be wrong."

"Aren't you the smart one? Why don't you have a plan?" Adelia snapped.

"I was too busy saving your life to come up with one in the last hour," Hero replied tartly.

Adelia didn't say anything—Hero was right, and they knew that they were right, and they didn't need her to tell them so. She bent slowly toward the water, pushing the thinning hyacinth aside to scoop up a hatful of relatively clear water. She poured it over herself, sluicing away fever-sweat. Abigail's tail flicked behind her, and for a few minutes, the only sound was the splash of Adelia's hat dipping into the water and tipping over her head.

Hero coughed. "Do you mind?" they said, and at first Adelia didn't know what they meant—but then she realized that they were close enough together on the saddle that Hero's back was soaked.

"Sorry, sorry," Adelia laughed, combing her wet hair

back from her face with her fingers before putting her hat back on. "I—I didn't think—"

"It's fine," Hero grumbled, and the set of their shoulders was so offended that Adelia burst out laughing again.

"I really am very sorry, Hero," she said. "I think the fever cooked my brain."

"It's alright," Hero said with a glance over their shoulder. "It's kind of nice. My back was getting mighty hot what with your feverish self trying hard to be a furnace back there. How are you feeling?"

"Like a trough of hop shit," Adelia said.

Hero chuckled to themself. "So, a bit better, then?"

"A bit," Adelia said, smiling. She tilted her head back and let the sun warm her damp face for a few minutes before returning her attention to the water. A ripple broke the surface, and she tensed, reaching for a blade to throw—but it was just a fish, reducing the number of water bugs on the creek by one.

"What about after?" Hero murmured, softly enough that Adelia wouldn't have heard it if Abigail hadn't stopped to investigate a toad in her path.

"What about it?" Adelia replied.

"What will you do, after we get Ysabel back?" Hero tugged on Abigail's harness, and the hippo waded forward again, leaving the relieved toad behind. "Will you go back into the wilderness and hide?"

Adelia shifted in the saddle. "No," she said, "I don't think so."

"Will you go back to work? What's going to happen?" Hero sounded oddly agitated. Adelia felt a heat rise in her scalp, and took off her hat to fan herself with it.

"No," she said, forcing her voice to be cold and flat so that she wouldn't yell. "I will not be going 'back to work.' That—that will never happen." Hero didn't say anything, and Adelia found herself wanting to continue in spite of—because of?—the sudden flush of anger. "I have not 'worked' in nearly a year now, Hero, did you know that? Did you know that it's been that long since I've taken a life?" She spat into the water. "A year. That's the longest I've gone since the first time. A year."

"I didn't know that," Hero murmured, their shoulders tense.

"I didn't even kill Travers," Adelia said, her pulse pounding in her ears. "I didn't even kill *you,* Dios ayúdame. I am—do you understand me? I am finished with it." Her fists were clenched tightly in her lap, and she could feel her fingernails driving crescents into her palms. "I am done with that."

"Sure," Hero said. "I hear you. You've retired." They got quiet, spoke in the slow cadence of someone finally coming to understand. "You didn't kill me."

"I've retired," Adelia repeated, flexing her fingers. "I am *retired*."

"Give you some advice?" Hero asked, then continued without waiting for Adelia's reply. "Find yourself something to do. Find a hobby. Otherwise . . . you get restless. Lonesome."

"Lonesome?" Adelia asked, holding back a sharp, bitter laugh. "I have been alone all my life, Hero. I don't think loneliness would be a problem for me."

"Alone and lonely ain't the same thing at all," Hero said, shaking their head. Adelia couldn't see their face, but it sounded as though the words hurt them. "You of all people should know that. And even if they were the same—you would think that being alone and retired would be no different from feeling alone in your job. But you'd be wrong."

"You wouldn't know a goddamn thing about it, Hero," Adelia snapped. "You may not be as infamous as Archie, but you have your own reputation, sí? You always worked in a team. It's why your hands have stayed so *soft*." She regretted it the instant she said it, but they both knew it was true—Hero was a behind-the-scenes type, a tinkerer, a poisoner. They had fingers made for capping vials and twisting wires together. They didn't have the knife scars ubiquitous to most hoppers, with one notable exception.

"Exactly," Hero murmured. "I've been hearing that my

whole life. It's lonesome being a killer, Adelia. But it's lonesome staying behind while the killers pour your poison into someone's drink, too. It's lonesome to be back at the ranch while someone else sets up the bombs you rigged. Don't tell me I don't know lonesome." Their voice was soft, but not sad. Not even angry. Just . . . resigned.

Adelia chewed on it—the idea of Hero being lonely. The idea of their bright mind—always working—growing bored in their retirement. She chewed on it, and perhaps it was her fever making her bold, but she finally asked the question that she had known all along she was not supposed to ask.

"Why did you retire?" she said. "Why not just . . . roughen your hands a bit?"

"Same reason as you," Hero said. "I got tired of killing people." Adelia started to protest, but Hero held up a hand. "Don't try to deny it. I heard you a minute ago—you're finished with it. You're done. I know how that is too."

"Oh?"

Hero spat into the water, then reached down to run a hand across Abigail's flank. "You kill the first one, and it's not as bad as you thought it would be. You kill the second one, and it's not better, not exactly. But it's more not-so-bad. You kill the third one and you realize that you're good at it." They scooped up a handful of water and splashed it across the hippo's shoulders, darkening her grey hide. "You start to get a reputation, and you realize that people think you're *great* at it. You start to take real pride in your work. You start to make real damn money." Another handful of water, this one across Abigail's neck. The hippo grunted appreciatively, flapping her ears. "You dream about contracts and you start tasting your own poisons to get a feel for how they land in the gut, and you love it. And then you're doing it *because* you love it, and you think you've really found your calling. You're so fucking *good* at this." They poured another handful of water between Abigail's ears, rubbing it across her skin with a long-fingered hand. "So you keep on mixing poisons and blasting vault doors open until you could do it in your sleep. And then one day, some kid shows up at your door and says that they've heard you're the best in the business, and you think—am I?"

Adelia didn't say anything, even as Hero's pause thickened.

"You realize," Hero finally said softly, "that you're only doing the job because you're good at it. That you only love it because you're good at it. You realize that somewhere along the way, you forgot that you're killing people. You don't feel a goddamn ounce of the remorse that your mother's preacher said you'd feel if you ever took another life—you just feel bored." Their voice dropped to a whisper. "You feel bored by the murders. And you wonder who you are, that you can say that about yourself—that you're bored by the murders."

Adelia swallowed hard, brushing away a mosquito that had come to investigate the tears that had traced trails to the hollow of her throat. She watched the sandy banks of Thompson Creek drift by—she spotted only a single feral sunning itself on the shore, so still that not even Abigail noticed it there. She lifted a fistful of muddy water to her face to wash away the salt and sweat that had accumulated. By the time her face was dry, Abigail was climbing up out of the creek and starting down the man-made stream that led to Whelan Parrish's barge.

Chapter 8

HOUNDSTOOTH'S HANDS WERE STEADY for the first time in nearly three months. He finally understood how the ferals must have felt when they slid up the Mississippi and found themselves free of the Harriet.

He felt good.

He twirled his favorite ivory-handled knife between his fingers like a baton, sober as mountain air, and strode in a slow circle around the ladder-backed chair. The chair was resting on its side on the sawdust-strewn floor. It was a well-made chair, Houndstooth mused. It had stood up to the impact of his boot when he'd kicked it over.

He couldn't say as much for the innkeeper tied to the chair, of course. No—that man's nose had taken the brunt of the impact when his face had hit the floor, and he was bleeding all over the place. The sawdust could only manage so much.

It would need to manage quite a lot more if the innkeeper didn't start answering questions soon.

"I can do this all night, Percival," Houndstooth said, letting his already-low voice drop to an even deeper baritone than usual. "You, on the other hand? I don't know if you'll be able to keep up with me." He crouched in front of the innkeeper, grabbing a fistful of the man's thinning, oiled hair. He pulled hard enough to lift Percival's head from the floor. Blood had pasted a good deal of sawdust to the man's cheek. "You're a mess," Houndstooth said, shaking his head slowly. He lifted his knife and used the edge to scrape Percival's cheek clean. "Oh, dear," he said. "My mistake. I seem to have taken some whiskers off of you." He wiped his knife on the innkeeper's shirtfront, then lifted it again. "I'll just even you up, shall I?" He scraped the blade against the man's other cheek, letting him feel just how sharp it was.

"I don't know where they went," Percival whimpered. Houndstooth dropped his head, and it bounced off the wooden floor with a crack.

"The problem here," Houndstooth said, twirling his knife again, "is that I don't believe you. I don't believe you because you do this . . . this *thing*." He tapped the tip of the blade against Percival's front teeth. "You bite your lip, see? Right before you tell me that lie."

"It's not a—what are you doing?" Percival's voice rose to a high quaver as Houndstooth grabbed the top of the ladder-backed chair with one hand, hauling it upright.

"Well, it's tricky, trying to look at you when you're all sideways down there, eh? That's no way to have a conversation," Houndstooth said. He brushed sawdust from his palms, then stooped to pick up his knife. He tossed it a few times, watching it flash as it spun through the air, savoring the clarity of purpose that had entered his mind at last.

"I don't enjoy being lied to," he said, pulling a second chair in front of Percival's. He rested one elbow on his knee and started paring his fingernails with the blade of the ivory-handled knife.

"Where's the marshal? And the other gentleman, your—um, your friend, from before?" The innkeeper kept glancing toward the stairs as though anyone could come walking down them who might save him.

"They're conferring." As he said it, a *thump* sounded from just above their heads, near the room that Hero and Adelia had been occupying until just a half hour before. "They have some catching up to do. It's none of my business, and it's *certainly* none of yours." He tapped the innkeeper's forehead. "Eyes on me, eh, Percival? Let's not try to eavesdrop, now. S'downright rude."

Percival reluctantly looked from the ceiling to the stairs, then to Houndstooth. The side of his face that had struck the floor was swelling; blood trickled from a cut over his eye, from his nose, from the corner of his mouth. *Disgraceful,* Houndstooth thought a bit giddily.

"What do you want?" Percival whispered. "I—I'll give

you—there's not much in the till, but it's yours. Please." His teeth found his lower lip again. "I don't know where they are."

Houndstooth's hand shot out. Before the innkeeper could so much as flinch, Houndstooth had the man's lip gripped between his thumb and index finger. He held tightly to it even as Percival thrashed like a fresh-caught catfish. It only took a few seconds for Percival's higher functions to cut off his instincts—when he was finally still, Houndstooth leaned in close enough that he could have kissed the little weasel on the nose. He smiled, not relinquishing his grip on the innkeeper's lower lip, and whispered to him as softly as a lover.

"You're a fucking liar, little man. You're trying to play a game to which you've never learned the rules. You're making mistakes." He tapped Percival on the teeth with the tip of his knife again. "You keep biting your fucking lip and then lying to me. So here's what's going to happen. Look at me, Percival," he said, and the innkeeper tore his eyes away from the stairs behind Houndstooth. His saliva was starting to drip down Houndstooth's wrist, but Houndstooth hardly noticed. He watched the other man's eyes like a bobcat watching a hare. "Here's what's going to happen. I'm going to cut off your lip—ah, ah, no no, hold still, now—" Percival had tried to yell, a wet, half-strangled noise. Houndstooth waited for the man to quiet down again; until his breaths started to come in short, shallow pants. "I'm going," Houndstooth began again, "to cut off your lip. That way, you'll have nothing to bite, and you'll have to tell the truth. How does that sound? Good?"

He lifted his knife and held it to the corner of Percival's lower lip. A sense of serenity—as deep and thorough as sleeping under the stars with Hero's hand resting on his chest—washed over him as he applied the faintest bit of pressure to the blade. After a few seconds, blood was running freely down his wrist, staining his shirtsleeve.

The tenor of the innkeeper's screaming changed abruptly, and he seemed to be attempting words. Houndstooth paused.

"What was that?" he asked, not looking up from the man's lip, which was still three-quarters attached. "If you keep interrupting, this will take forever, you know." Percival's response was unintelligible, since he couldn't move his lip or jaw. "That sounded a bit like 'I'll tell you everything,'" Houndstooth said. "Was that what you were saying, Percival, old friend?"

Percival nodded, then screamed as the motion of his head drove Houndstooth's knife further into his lip.

"Excellent!" Houndstooth released the innkeeper's lip and drew the knife back in one fluid movement, eliciting another scream. "I knew we could come to an understanding." He smiled, wiped his blade on Percival's sleeve, and set it aside.

"I don't—don't hurt me, please, I'll tell you everything I know. But I don't know exactly where they went." He spoke in a rush. *Motivated at last,* Houndstooth thought, and he felt his smile grow wider. "I just know who sent for them. But you have to swear you won't tell him that I'm the one who told you—he'll kill me, or he'll have someone else kill me, please, you have to promise me—"

Houndstooth propped his foot on the edge of Percival's chair, leaning back in his chair and folding his arms. "And who, pray tell," he asked softly, "might that have been?"

"'Oundstooth? What are you—mon dieu. 'Oundstooth!"

Houndstooth rolled his neck, letting out an involuntary sigh. "Just a minute, Archie," he called over his shoulder—but it was too late. Archie was already rushing up behind him. He braced himself for the warm weight of her hand on his shoulder, half longing for the contact and half dreading it.

"Help, please, he's lost his mind," Percival began to whimper, slurring the words over his mangled lip. Archie stood beside Houndstooth, not touching him, and took in the scene.

"I most certainly *have* lost my mind," Houndstooth said, his eyes fixed on the innkeeper. "Who knows what I'm liable to do next, if you don't give me that name?"

"'Oundstooth." Houndstooth held up a hand. Archie grabbed his arm and yanked until he faced her. "You've gone too far, 'Oundstooth. *No*—" She held up a finger, hissing so quietly that the man in the chair leaned forward to hear, dripping blood onto Houndstooth's boot. "Is this what you think they would want from you? Is this what you think they would ask you to do for them? Is this what you think they want you to be, when they're not around to tether you to your humanity? Mon dieu, 'Oundstooth," she whispered, shaking her head. "You 'ave become a *demon*."

Houndstooth wiped sweat from his top lip with a shirtsleeve. His hand had the slightest of tremors. He eyed it with suspicion. "We can ask them in person, Archie, my friend. Percival here was just about to tell me who's housing Adelia. And Hero."

Out of the corner of his eye, Houndstooth could tell that Archie was watching him, evaluating. He knew that she was weighing his behavior over the last two months against all that she knew about him. He gritted his teeth and turned to meet her eyes, schooling the fury from his face. He smoothed himself to a semblance of his usual wry calm, raising an eyebrow at his flushed friend. She studied his face for a few long seconds, then nodded. "Don't let me interrupt, then, by all means," she said, waving a decorous hand at Percival.

Houndstooth gave her a smile, which she didn't return. Then he returned his attention to the limp, bleeding man in the ladder-backed chair. He tapped Percival's lower lip with the nail of his pinky finger. "Well?"

Behind him, footsteps pounded down the stairs. He ignored them—ignored the sound of Archie explaining things to Carter in a low murmur, ignored the sound of them whispering about him. None of it mattered, because Percival was finally gathering his courage.

"Alright—okay. The girl who delivered the message. She works for a lot of folks—steals from a lot of folks too, knocks over taverns from time to time. It's why I let her work out of my bar, see? I figured, if this was her base of operations . . ."

Houndstooth shifted in his chair, raising an eyebrow and making a rolling "get on with it" motion with one hand. Percival took a shuddering breath.

"The man she's been running for most often lately is named Whelan Parrish. He's a federal—"

Houndstooth didn't realize he'd risen to his feet until he heard his chair hit the floor. "A federal agent with the Bureau of Land Management," he finished, and Percival gaped at him for a moment before nodding.

"Yes, he's a—he's with the Bureau of Land Management, how did you . . . ?"

Houndstooth snatched his hat from his head and threw it to the ground. It landed in the pasty puddle of sawdust and blood near Percival's feet. "Son of a whoring hop-shitted *fuck,*" Houndstooth spat.

"Did he say Parrish?"

Houndstooth turned on his heel and stalked toward the foot of the stairs where Carter stood. "Yes, *Carter,* yes, he said *Parrish.* I believe you're acquainted?"

Carter didn't flinch, even as Houndstooth came close enough to him that their noses nearly touched. He placed a firm but gentle hand on Houndstooth's chest, applying just enough pressure to put a few inches between them.

"I corresponded with him several months ago about the Harriet job," he said, his voice low and even. Houndstooth's pulse pounded in his ears—he wanted Carter to hit him, wanted to fight him, wanted anything but this calm, cool response.

And then, of course, it got worse.

"From what I understand," Carter continued in that unbearably soothing tone, "you know him better than anyone else in this room, Houndstooth."

"Who the 'ell are you two going on about?" Archie demanded.

Houndstooth closed his eyes and took a deep, slow

breath. He answered Archie with his eyes closed. He could handle Hero's disappearance—could handle the weeks of searching, and the sleepless nights, and the wondering if they were even alive. But somehow, the idea of looking at Archie in that moment was nearly enough to break him.

"We're talking about Whelan fucking Parrish," Houndstooth said, failing to keep his voice level. "The federal agent who hired us for the Harriet job."

Archie didn't quite succeed in holding back a gasp. "'Oundstooth—do you mean—"

"Yes, Archie."

"But isn't he—"

"*Yes,* Archie."

"But didn't you two—"

Behind them, there was a clatter as Percival finally fainted, knocking his ladder-backed chair to the floor and crushing Houndstooth's best grey hat. Houndstooth gritted his teeth hard enough to make his jaw ache. "Yes, Archie," he said. "The man who's got Hero and Adelia right now is Whelan Parrish, federal agent for the Bureau of Land Management. My blue-eyed boy."

Chapter 9

HERO WATCHED FROM UNDER the brim of their hat as a bead of sweat traced its way down Adelia's temple. They wondered how much longer she'd last.

They shifted their weight against the white-painted wainscoting in Whelan Parrish's parlor and scanned the room again, letting their eyes skip over the white-blond man seated across from Adelia.

"You're an idiot, Mister Parrish." Adelia brushed the bead of sweat away with a remarkably steady hand. Her voice was even. A little too even. *Keep it together, Adelia,* they thought. *Just stay upright until he's gone.* "I had already guessed that you were a fool—you would have to be, to invite us to your home. But it appears that I overestimated you."

"Oh?" Parrish ashed his pipe into a tall, fluted vase next to his rocking chair. "How do you figure?"

"Adelia's retired," Hero murmured. They said it just quietly enough that Parrish could have pretended not to hear them—but he didn't.

"I don't give a piping hot damn," Parrish drawled, not

looking away from Adelia. "She's coming out of retirement tonight."

Adelia's head snapped up. Hero had pushed off the wall and was standing between Parrish and Adelia before they knew what they were doing. "Tonight?" they snapped, louder than they'd intended.

Parrish smiled, showing a row of teeth that were so even they couldn't be real. Hippo ivory, probably, and recently fitted at that. Hero wanted to knock them out of his mouth.

"Tonight," he said, leaning over to look at Adelia. "You'll kill Mr. Burton tonight. Or I'll throw your baby into the Mississippi and let the ferals crush her soft little skull between their teeth."

Adelia didn't make a sound. Hero didn't turn to look at her—couldn't turn to look at her, couldn't risk the appearance of concern.

"Why tonight?" they demanded. "Why can't it wait for us to make a real plan?"

Parrish finally looked at Hero, his lip curling. His eyes were a startlingly bright blue, incongruous in his dishwater complexion. "Tonight is Mr. Burton's seventy-eighth birthday," he sneered. "He'll be feted here on the *Duchess*. There will be drinking and dancing and toasts and gifts and then do you know what will happen?" He waited, staring at Hero with lead-weighted malice writ plainly across his features.

"What? What will happen then?"

"He'll go back to the Bureau of Land Management headquarters in Atlanta. He'll sit behind his desk and he'll continue running the bureau into the ground, and I'll rot underneath him until the day I die." Parrish pulled at his pipe, fuming smoke.

Hero laughed, incredulous. "You must be joking," they said. "All this is for a job?" They shook their head and ran a hand across their face. "You kidnapped a baby for—what? For a *promotion*?"

Parrish leveled a cold stare at Hero. "I kidnapped the baby for the well-being of this country," he said. "Burton is the damned fool who let the Hippo Bill through."

"Congress let the Hippo Bill through," Adelia rasped from behind Hero. "The Senate let the Hippo Bill through. President—"

"No," Parrish shouted, jabbing his pipe at Adelia. "They let the Hippo Bill become a *law*! Burton let it *through*! There are so many ways he could have stopped it—so many—you can delay *anything,"* he sputtered, then closed his mouth with a click of those false teeth. His jaw worked as he breathed heavily through flared nostrils. After a moment, he closed his eyes and ran a hand over his slicked-back hair, taking deep, slow breaths. Hero watched, fascinated, as he continued

stroking his own hair, growing visibly calmer with each pass of his pale hand. "The man loves hippos," he muttered. "He thinks they're delightful. He let the bill *through* because he is an *idiot*. He'll never approve the extermination of the American variant of the species. And I can't for the life of me get him *fired*. If that disaster at the Harriet couldn't do it—no, this is the only way." He opened his eyes and nodded to Adelia. "So you'll kill him, *tonight,* and I'll be promoted into his position, and I'll clean up the mess he left behind."

"How?" Hero asked. "The hippos are here to stay. What can you do that he can't?"

"It's not what I can do that he can't," Parrish said. "It's what I will do that he *won't*. Those beasts are a menace, and he thinks they should be treated like—like *deer*!" His eyes narrowed. "I think they should be treated like the vermin that they are. And when I'm in charge of the bureau, I'll be able to declare a state of emergency, bringing the full might of the United States military down upon the Hippo Problem. We'll wipe them out within a few months, at the most. Each and every one. The farms will be shut down, and this long, embarrassing chapter in our nation's history will be over at last." He sniffed, smoothing his hair again, then muttered, "That includes your little pets, by the way. Enjoy them while they last."

Hero blinked. Their face felt numb. "You can't kill the

livestock, too," they said. "That's insane, Parrish. It's madness. People will starve."

Parrish grinned, suddenly looking like a cat with feathers in its teeth. "People will have jobs."

"What?"

He ran a tongue over his teeth, then spoke to Hero in a tone that implied he was uncertain of their ability to understand. "I am currently the owner of ninety percent of the boats that are on the Mississippi, the Ponchartrain, and the Ohio River." He fondled the corner of a waxed leather folio that rested on his desk. "I'd like to be able to *operate* them. Once the vermin is out of the water, I'll be able to do so. Do you comprehend this?"

Hero shook their head. "Travers seemed to think that having the hippos in the water made his work quite a bit easier."

"Yes, well, Travers was a sadistic simpleton," Parrish snapped. "I'd rather not have to replenish my staff due to *grisly deaths*. His empire was one of blood and sweat." Parrish stood, tugging at the bottom of his waistcoat. "Mine will be one of money."

He gave Adelia a final, appraising look. "You have ten hours until the party begins, Miss Reyes." He jerked his chin toward a small silver bell that rested on the table next to his chair. "Ring that when you're ready, and my staff will show you to your quarters for the evening."

"What about me?" Hero asked.

"What about you?" Parrish snapped at them, his face reddening again. "I didn't send for you. I sent for *her*. You were not invited to this party, and I can't imagine a use for you. You're lucky I don't have you shot for trespassing on my property."

"Hero is with me," Adelia said, pushing herself up out of her chair. "They're my partner, and where I go, they go. And if you harm them, I will slit you open like a letter and read the contents to the river."

Parrish shook his head at Adelia. "I'd been told that you work alone. You're *supposed* to work alone."

"Your opinion is not of interest to me," she replied. "Now, if you'll excuse us. We have a plan to pull out of our asses."

Parrish stalked from the room, his pipe clenched in one white-knuckled fist. The instant the door had slammed shut behind him, Adelia collapsed back into her chair.

"Pollas en vinagre," she murmured, pressing her hands to her face.

Hero stared at her. "Partner, eh?"

"Sorry," Adelia groaned. "I was—it seemed like the right thing to say. I don't know. Manda huevos. Ten hours?"

Hero eased themself into the rocking chair Parrish

had recently vacated, trying to ignore how warm the seat still was. They imagined Abigail, Ruby, Rosa, Zahra, Stasia—all dead, along with every hippo ever bred on U.S. soil. They couldn't wrap their head around it. "We'll figure it out."

"What did we bring with us?" Adelia asked, eyes still closed. "Just the one bag, right?"

"I grabbed what I could," Hero said. It had been a frenzy—they had shoved everything they could see into the bag, tossed it out the window. Some things had surely fallen out as they'd tried to half carry, half drag Adelia through the back alleys of Baton Rouge and along the winding road to Port Rouge. "And let's see—I've got . . ." They turned out their pockets, dropping a few paper-padded vials on the table, along with a waxed brick of explosive putty the size of a deck of playing cards.

"Plus your knives, plus my knives," Adelia murmured, kneading her temple with her fingers. "Ah, my head is *bellowing*."

"Why don't we take a look at our 'quarters,'" Hero ventured. "Maybe you can get some rest? We've been traveling all day."

"There's no time," Adelia breathed, but her eyes didn't open.

"We'll plan after you've had a nap and I've had a bath," Hero said. "Nine hours isn't that much less than ten."

They stood a few feet from Adelia and held out a hand. After a moment, Adelia cracked one eye, evaluated the hand—and took it. Hero helped her out of her chair.

"Alright," Adelia said. "Alright. One hour. But only because you wanted a bath."

"Oh, trust me, you could use one too," Hero said, reaching for the bell with a grin. "But I get to go first. *Partner.*"

~

The bath was everything Hero had hoped it would be, which is to say the water was warm and mostly clear. There was even soap, and it was good soap, with some kind of smell to it. Hero couldn't put their finger on the smell, but it smelled much better than anything they'd been smelling over the last two months, so they lathered themself with it until their skin squeaked.

On the other side of a painted silk screen, Adelia was asleep. Hero knew that Adelia was still asleep because she wasn't muttering to herself about how she wasn't tired and resting was a waste of time. They endeavored to get out of the tub quietly—although they doubted that any amount of noise would rouse Adelia now—and reached for the length of linen that had been left for them to dry off with. It wasn't exactly soft, but it didn't scratch and it wasn't dry clothes over wet skin, which was nice.

Hurried footsteps sounded in the hall, and Hero pulled the towel around themself. They opened the door, startling the hell out of the maid who was about to knock on it.

"Oh! Oh, I'm sorry, I—uh, they told me—there was a lady staying here? Miss Reyes?" The maid blew a lock of curly red hair out of her face.

"She's resting. Did you need something from her?"

The maid held out another length of linen, this one folded into a thick packet. She spoke so quickly that Hero could barely keep up. "The chef for tonight sent these. She's, um. She lost a baby last month and she had some problems and the butler—he showed you up here?—well, he talked to her about what's going on with Miss Reyes and she said it sounds like Miss Reyes has the same problems she had. I don't know what she's talking about, but she said to bring this to y'all."

Hero took the cloth from the girl and unfolded it. They could hear Adelia stirring behind them. "Cabbage leaves?"

The maid shrugged. "She said to put 'em on Miss Reyes's, uh, 'inflamed areas.'" She started to edge away down the hall with the unmistakable air of someone who does not wish to discuss the matter any further. "Good luck!"

When Adelia had applied the cabbage leaves—a scene Hero did not witness, as they chose instead to take their time getting dressed behind the silk screen—she seemed to brighten. "I don't know if it's working or not," she said, "but they're cold, at least."

"Aha," Hero said, because there was not a single other thing they could think of to say. Adelia was sitting upright in the bed, and Hero perched awkwardly at the end of it.

"So," Adelia said. "The plan."

"Right. The plan. I took an inventory, and we have a good variety of poisons, although—"

"No." Adelia pulled her hair off of her neck and fanned herself with the flat of her hand. Her eyes were still worryingly glassy. "The plan for after."

"What?" Hero wondered if perhaps Adelia needed another hour of sleep before she would be coherent.

"We don't need a plan for the murder, Hero," Adelia said. "It will be simple. I will walk into the party and slit this 'Burton' fellow's throat. Or I'll hit him between the eyes with a throwing knife. Or I'll find a curtain tie and garrote him." She was studying the backs of her hands as she spoke, her eyes tracing the network of tiny scars that mapped them. "I will kill him the same way I would kill anyone else. No elaborate plan required."

"But how will we get him alone?" Hero shook their head. "You're not making any sense. You can't just walk into the middle of a party and kill a man—a *government official*. You'd hang."

"I'll hang anyway," Adelia murmured. She looked up at Hero, and her eyes were the clearest they'd been in days. "Gran Carter will find us, Hero. Yes? He has found us already. He will find me here—he is probably on his way already. And then he will capture me, and I will hang anyway. So I may as well do this job quickly."

"But—I don't understand," Hero said desperately. "I mean, I understand, but I don't—you're just giving up?"

Adelia smiled—a tired smile, but a warm one. A real one. "No," she said. "I'm not giving up. I'm making a plan." She looked back down at her hands, and Hero realized that they were seeing Adelia differently than they'd ever seen her. Even when she was about to give birth, Adelia had never seemed *nervous* before.

A cold finger of fear traced the scar just below Hero's navel.

"Hero," Adelia said. "I am going to kill Burton at the party, and then Parrish's demands will be met. Very shortly thereafter, Carter will capture me. I cannot outrun him, not like this." She gestured to herself—to her sweat-soaked hair, and to the damp patches over each breast where the cabbage leaves had made the fabric of her shirt cling. "I'm very sick, and I cannot run on my own. So . . . Carter will capture me, yes? We know this. And I will hang."

"But—"

"Let me finish," Adelia said softly. Hero bit their lip hard. They didn't want to hear the rest of this—there had to be another way. "I'm going to hang, but before I do . . . you can get Ysabel back from Parrish. He'll hand her off—he won't want to keep her, not once I'm captured and the job is done. He'll give her to you. And I need you to take her.

"Hero, I haven't—hm. How to say it? My life, for the past fifteen years, has been all about running. In all that time, I haven't trusted anyone but myself. That is"—she swallowed hard, still staring at her hands—"I haven't trusted anyone until these last two months. You had every reason to hate me—to *kill* me, even—but you didn't. You stayed with me. You helped me birth Ysabel, and you've helped me with her when you had no place helping me with anything. You've saved my life more times than I think you know." She cleared her throat. Hero blinked back hot tears; this was easily the longest they'd ever heard Adelia speak, and she was saying more than they could take in.

"You've been a friend to me, Hero. You've done so much for me, and now . . . I have to ask you for more."

Hero shook their head. "Don't," they whispered.

Adelia looked up at them, her eyes brimming.

"Promise me you'll take care of Ysabel," Adelia whispered. "Tell her—" Tears spilled onto her cheeks, and instead of wiping them away, she reached out and grabbed Hero's hands. "Tell her I was a murderer, that's—she should know that, she should know why I'm gone. Tell her I was the best. She should know that, too." Adelia smiled even as her tears splashed onto Hero's hands. "But tell her this. Tell her that I was every inch her mother, and that I loved her more than I loved being the best."

She squeezed Hero's hands so hard that the bones creaked. Hero felt themself nodding, even as an ache filled their chest. "I'll tell her," they said.

Adelia nodded back, once. She released Hero's hands and wiped at her face with the linen the cabbage had been wrapped in. "Alright," she said with a loud sniff. "That's settled, then." She swung her legs over the side of the bed and stood unsteadily.

"Where are you going?" Hero asked, rubbing the collar of their shirt across their cheeks. It felt so sudden—the conversation was over, and their future was decided.

"If I'm going to meet Gran Carter tonight," Adelia called as she stepped behind the silk screen, "I'd like to at least be clean. I hope you saved me some soap for my last bath on this earth, eh, Hero?"

"You should have told me you were planning to die a little sooner," Hero called back. Their voice was still thick with emotion, but they managed to laugh as a cabbage leaf came flying over the top of the screen at them. "What am I supposed to do with this?"

"Shove it up your ass," Adelia shot back. "And then go find me a fresh bar of soap."

Chapter 10

ARCHIE DIPPED HER FINGERTIPS into the water and ran them across her hairline for the thousandth time, smoothing down the wisps of hair that seemed determined to curl at her temples in the humidity of the late-afternoon air.

"You look beautiful," Carter murmured, in a voice so low that only she would be able to hear it.

"Beautiful is not what I'm worried about," Archie replied, but she smiled at him anyway. "But merci."

"What *are* you worried about, then?"

Archie looked over at Carter, struck as always by how unconscionably handsome he was. The low, golden sun made his features almost glow. His rented hippo, Antoinette, was too small for him—the water nearly lapped his knees—but he rode with a grace that would have made anyone think he was a full-time hopper. "Getting into the party," she said. "You'll 'ave no problem—all you need to do is flash your star. And 'Oundstooth . . ." She glanced over her shoulder and ran out of words.

Houndstooth looked like himself again. And when he looked like himself, no party would turn him away, whether he had an invitation or not.

He'd changed into a suit that Archie had never seen him wear. She supposed he'd been saving it for a special occasion. She'd asked him if perhaps he wanted to change into it once they arrived at Parrish's barge, but he'd said that it would weather the ride there. So far, it had; the crisp collar of his plum shirt still stood tall and contrasted his white four-in-hand brilliantly, sending a tart spark of envy across Archie's tongue. He'd shaved and trimmed his own hair in the time it had taken for Archie to arm herself and oil the chain of her meteor hammer; he was immaculately combed, his moustache waxed into a razor curl. There was a light in his eyes—the light of expectation. The light of hope.

He winked at her from his seat astride Ruby's back, and Archie's heart nearly broke with relief.

"Why wouldn't you be able to get in?" Carter said, breaking into Archie's thoughts.

"I will," Archie replied. "I will. I suppose I am just worried about what would happen if I didn't."

Carter nudged Antoinette close enough to bump into Rosa. Rosa gave a snort, spraying creekwater over Antoinette's jowls, but didn't move away. "We won't be separated again, Archie," Carter said. "I mean it. I'm not going to run off chasing Adelia. This time, if I don't get her—and I *will* get her," he added, narrowing his eyes, "—but if I don't get her, I'm not going to run off after her. I swear."

"Don't make promises," Archie said with a sad smile. "Just keep them."

"Archie." Carter shifted on Antoinette's back, probably sore from spending so many hours in the saddle already. "I know you don't like me to make promises, but . . . I've been wanting to talk to you about maybe making some plans."

Archie stared straight ahead, watching the ripples in the water. "We 'ave a plan. We'll go to the party, find Adelia, arrest her, and let Winslow have ten minutes alone with her to find out where 'Ero is."

"That's not what I—"

A piercing whistle cut him off. Archie and Carter both looked back to see Houndstooth staring at the water a few hundred feet away. He'd gone stock-still. One hand gripped the pommel of Ruby's saddle; with the other, he was reaching for the fully assembled harpoon that was strapped across his back. Archie started to call out to ask him what was the matter, but he raised a hand without looking away from the patch of water his eyes were fixed upon, and she fell silent.

For a long, tense minute, the only sound was Rosa

blowing bubbles in the murky brown water. Finally, Houndstooth lowered his hand, shaking his head. He rode up next to Archie and Carter, still watching that patch of water.

"What is it?" Archie asked, looking between her old friend and the place he was staring at.

"I don't know," Houndstooth replied. "I thought I saw something—a wake—but then it was gone."

Archie patted Rosa's flank, and the three of them picked up speed, riding abreast through the widening creek. "A breeze, perhaps?"

"No, it was bigger than—never mind." Houndstooth rolled his shoulders. "I'm sure it was nothing."

"It's good of you to be so vigilant," Carter said. "You've got a keen eye, Houndstooth. We could use men like you in the service."

Houndstooth laughed and drew breath to say something that would probably make Carter regret his invitation, but stopped before saying anything, his head cocked.

"What is it now?" Archie asked, not unkindly.

"Do you hear that?" Houndstooth said, a smile spreading across his features.

"No, but then, my hearing isn't what it used to be. What is it?" Carter asked, looking around at the surface of the water. The three of them rounded a bend in the creek, and then Archie heard it: a faint ragtime melody that grew a little louder as Ruby, Rosa, and Antoinette proceeded through the water. After a moment, Carter heard it too—his face grew stern, and as Archie watched, a mantle of authority seemed to settle over his shoulders.

"That'll be the party, then," he said. One of his hands drifted up to check that his marshal's star was affixed firmly to the brim of his hat.

"Almost there," Houndstooth said with a giddy grin.

Archie didn't say anything at all. She checked that the chain of her meteor hammer was properly coiled. She loosened the straps on the knives that were sheathed at her shoulders, her waist, and her thighs. She unbuttoned the top button of her blouse. Then she leaned over, dipped her fingertips in the water, and smoothed her hair down again. Just in case.

~

The barge was bigger than Archie could have anticipated. The narrow stream that led up to it was too straight to be anything but man-made, so she'd known there was money at work, but it wasn't until she saw the thing for herself that she realized how *much* money. It was a floating mansion in the middle of a perfectly round private pond. Three ferrymen poled finely appointed party guests from the shore to the deck of the barge, where they were helped up by a servant in a coat and tails.

And there were so many guests. At least a hundred that Archie could see, and judging from the noise, twice that already inside. A loud cheer went up from somewhere within, followed by the sound of shattering glass and another round of shouts. Above it all, the music continued unabated—a powerful piano pounding out "The Wild Pottamus Rag." It was Archie's least favorite of the songs that had been written about the collapse of the Harriet Dam, not least because of the chorus: "And not a soul escaped alive, and not a soul escaped alive, hi-ho hop-whoa! And everybody died."

Not everybody, asshole, she thought tartly.

"Excuse me." A ferryman was stepping out of his boat and approaching them. Archie rested an easy hand on the hilt of the knife that hung at her waist. Out of the corner of her eye, she saw Carter slip the strap off his pistol with all the smooth subtlety of a gator sliding into the water.

"Yes?" Houndstooth said in an easy, friendly voice.

"I'll need to see your invitation, please," the ferryman said. "And you'll need to leave your hippopotami with the pondhand." He snapped his fingers at a skinny, towheaded white boy in wading boots. Archie flinched, remembering another skinny boy who had wanted to be a hopper. She looked away from the pondhand before she could remember too hard.

"Of course," Houndstooth said, reaching into the breast pocket of his waistcoat. He paused, cocked his head, and reached into his other pocket. He made a show of checking his jacket, then swore. "Damn," he said, frowning at Archie. "You don't have our invitations, do you?"

"You were supposed to bring them," Archie said. She glanced at Carter, who nodded, then looked back at Houndstooth. "Don't tell me you don't have them at all, 'Oundstooth?"

He patted himself down, then shrugged. "I must have left them on the chifforobe." He looked up at the ferryman with a half smile. "I'm so sorry, my friend, I appear to have forgotten them."

"Alas," the ferryman said drily. "I can't let you in without one. Are you *certain* that you don't have an invitation? Just one would do for all three of you."

Houndstooth stared at him for a beat, then broke into a broad grin. "Oh, yes, of course. How could I forget?" He reached into his breast pocket again, and this time, he withdrew a bulging paper packet, tied with twine. "Here they are."

The ferryman took the packet and weighed it in his hand before nodding to Houndstooth. "Very good, sir." He snapped to the pondhand again, and the boy came running. "You may leave your hippos with Arthur and retrieve them again at the end of the evening."

"We'll take them around back ourselves, thank you," Carter said. The ferryman raised an eyebrow at him, but then, glancing up at the star on his hat, nodded.

"Very good, Mister Marshal," he said. He gave them directions to the paddock, then turned smartly away, greeting a set of guests that had arrived overland.

Archie guided Rosa into the pond, patting the hippo's white flank. "You were very brave back there, chérie," she cooed. Rosa's ears flipped back and forth as she slid into the clear water of the private pond. A cloud of mud bloomed from her hide, muddying the water around her. "Very brave," Archie added in a murmur.

The paddock was a loosely constructed ring of buoys with netting strung between them. As Archie, Houndstooth, and Carter approached, a second pondhand untied a length of netting and drew it aside. A few hippos were inside already, their ears and noses barely breaking the surface of the water. One flicked an ear at Ruby as she slid between the buoys and into the paddock, ahead of Rosa. Houndstooth pulled Ruby up short, much as he had in Thompson Creek, and stared.

"It can't be," he whispered.

"What's the holdup?" Carter called from behind Archie. Houndstooth ignored him, urging Ruby toward the hippo that had caught his attention—a runty grey one that had clocked Ruby as she entered the paddock.

"That's . . . that's Abigail," Houndstooth said. At the sound of her name, Abigail lifted her great grey head out of the water. "That's *Abigail*."

Carter looked at Archie. "Hero's girl, Abigail?"

Archie nodded as Houndstooth took his hat off, running a hand through his hair. "I thought we left her back at Port Rouge," she said.

"We did," Houndstooth replied. "Or . . . I don't know, I thought we did. It was dark, we were in such a hurry, I didn't think to check—" He rubbed his eyes with one hand, looking old for a moment. "This doesn't make any sense at all. How would Hero have gotten ahold of her?"

"Are you sure it's her?" Archie asked. Houndstooth nodded slowly, then pulled himself up onto the dock that led from the paddock to the barge. Without looking back, he stalked toward the sound of the party.

"Will he be okay in there?" Carter asked as Archie dismounted.

"We'll find out," Archie said, staring at Houndstooth's back as the sound of his red hippo-leather boots pounding on the wood of the dock blended into the ragtime rhythm. "One way or the other."

~

The inside of the barge was dense with people. The crowd fairly bristled with knives, pistols, and fists. Archie pushed her way through, Carter at her back, and found Houndstooth standing at the entrance to the formal dining room. The long table was crowded with gifts, as thick as ticks on a dog's back—baskets of oranges, pistols shining with oil, long parcels wrapped in white paper. At the head of the table, the oldest man Archie had ever seen was hunched over a package, picking at the twine that wrapped it with a gnarled finger. He squinted at the knot with cloudy eyes, shaking his head, before pulling out a pocket knife and sawing through the twine. A young woman stood beside him with a sheaf of paper and an ivory-barreled pen; behind her was a stack of already-opened gifts, including an ill-advised model of the Harriet Dam as it had looked before it fell.

The young woman with the pen looked up just as Archie edged into the room, and Archie had to swallow a surprised laugh. It was Acadia, wearing a pile of false curls and a heavily ruffled corset that had pushed her bony frame into the approximate shape of a violin—all extravagant curves. She gave Archie a wicked grin before laying a possessive hand on the shoulder of the old man in the chair.

"I suppose that must be Mr. Burton," Archie said to Houndstooth, nodding to the old man. But Houndstooth didn't answer. Archie turned and found that he was no longer standing beside her. She whipped around, only to see him crossing the room, pushing people out of his way. A woman cried out as he shouldered past her, knocking her into a butler's tray of tall cocktail glasses.

"It's her," Carter said behind Archie. He was staring over the heads of the people in the crowd. "It must be. He must have seen Adelia—" Archie didn't want to hear more. She followed in Houndstooth's wake, stepping over the ankle of a man he'd bowled over, lifting her skirt to step over a puddle of gin on the floor. The quarters were too close for her to use her meteor hammer without putting the drunken party guests in danger, so she unsheathed her weightiest blade and shoved past a tall woman who had stepped into her path.

And then she saw Houndstooth. Some of the guests had wised up, clearing a path in front of the harpoon-strapped madman who was knocking people down. As Archie watched, her friend reached up and took his much-abused hat off, letting it fall behind him without so much as a backward glance. He strode forward and, as the crowd parted in front of him, grabbed one of the party guests by the shoulder.

They turned around.

Archie stopped in her tracks, feeling her mouth fall open, and stared. The music was too loud for her to make out everything Houndstooth was saying, but she didn't need to hear a word. Carter caught up to her just in time to watch with her as Houndstooth swept Hero into his arms. The air in the room stilled as he kissed them with the unrestrained fire of a man possessed by months of fear and searching and need and a tenacious, undying certainty that the person he loved was still out there, waiting for his lips to meet theirs.

"Oh," Carter said.

"Yes," Archie agreed.

"Excuse me," came a voice from beside her. Archie moved aside—out of the corner of her eye, she saw the tall, dark-haired woman she'd pushed aside a few moments before. The woman moved past, trailing the sharp smell of sweat and something sour.

Archie glanced back at the woman.

Then she looked again.

"Shit." She looked back at Houndstooth, who was holding Hero by the face, his forehead pressed to theirs. She looked up at Carter, who was watching the reunion with a familiar smile. "Fucking shit-arsed *fuck,*" she said, and grabbed Carter by the elbow. She started to pull him after her, following the path of the dark-haired woman. Behind her, she heard Houndstooth calling.

She looked over her shoulder, met his eyes, and nodded. As she turned back, she saw him cast a regretful glance at Hero. She didn't need to watch to know that he was following her.

"What is it?" Carter asked beside her.

"It's her," Archie answered, gathering a length of chain in one hand and tightening her grip on her still-unsheathed blade in the other. "It's Adelia."

Chapter 11

ADELIA'S HEAD SWAM. She heard a commotion behind her—but there was no time. Her fever was spiking again, her vision tunneling, and it was now or never.

Burton had to die.

She wove through the crowd, which seemed far too large for a government official's birthday party. She supposed that Parrish must have padded out the list with whoever he was accepting bribes from. She shook her head hard, trying to jar herself into focusing. *None of that matters,* she thought as she reached the door to the formal dining room. *None of it.* All that mattered was killing Burton and getting Ysabel into Hero's hands before—

A hand on her elbow.

No, she thought desperately. She shook off the hand and shoved her way into the dining room, barreling toward the head of the table. Burton looked up at her, his thick brows furrowed. She grabbed a length of cut twine from the table in front of him and stepped behind him in one fluid motion. A bead of fever-sweat ran down her back as she looped the twine around her palms, slipping it over the old man's head.

Now.

She heard the impact at first, more than she felt it—a crack from just behind her. She almost turned to look, but then she was falling, and a searing pain was in the back of her skull.

I've been shot, she thought. As she landed on the waxed wood of the dining room floor, she reached up with one hand, and felt her unbroken skull.

Not shot, then. She fought to remain conscious and won by the skin of her teeth. She started trying to scramble to her feet, but then hands were under her arms, and she was kicking as she was dragged back through the crowd, away from her only hope of getting Ysabel back.

~

"You can't," Hero was saying. Adelia tugged at the cuffs that Carter had applied to her wrists. The chain rattled against the chair to which she was tethered, and everyone turned to look at her.

"Please," she rasped, staring at Hero. "You have to do it. You have to kill him. Please." She was drenched in sweat, her head pounding—her fever had finally broken, too late to matter. She couldn't reach back to feel whether

her head was swelling where Carter had struck her, but she could guess.

"Why the hop-eared fuck would Hero do a thing like that?" Houndstooth growled, trying to lean back against a wall, then shifting again as his harpoon dug into his back. "This useless bloody thing, I swear—"

"Hero would do a thing like that," Hero said, making Houndstooth startle, "because it's the only way to get Ysabel back."

"And Ysabel is the baby, right?" Carter asked, pinching the bridge of his nose.

"I just don't understand why Parrish would kidnap Ysabel instead of just *hiring Adelia,*" Archie said. She was leaning against the plaster wall of the quarters that had been assigned to Adelia ten hours before.

"Because I'm retired," Adelia said. "He tried to hire me a year ago, and I told him no. And then he tried again, right before the Harriet job, and I told him no. And then he tried to sabotage the Harriet job, so that Burton would look incompetent and get fired, and he wanted me to help him do it—and I said no then, too. I think he went through Travers after that. And . . . then Travers decided to go through me anyway. I kept saying no, Hero. They kept trying to make me kill, and I kept saying no." She closed her eyes, wishing there was a way that she could will herself unconscious. "And men like him . . . they do not like to hear that word." At least then she would be able to get some sleep before hanging.

She could hear Houndstooth pacing back and forth in front of her with the measured steps of terrible patience. "And you were 'retired' when you tried to kill Hero?" His voice was quiet enough to make her open her eyes again—a dangerous kind of quiet that sent a rare spark of fear through her.

"That's what I'm trying to tell you, Houndstooth," Hero said. They grabbed him by both shoulders, staring into his eyes. "Adelia didn't try to kill me. She saved me. Do you understand? That's why it's so important that she's retired. She *didn't kill me*. If she hadn't done what she did—Travers would have killed me himself. I was the one who was setting up explosives in the Harriet, wasn't I?" They shook their head. "He would have made *sure* I was dead long before the dam fell."

"Hero, please," Adelia said. "None of that matters. Parrish has Ysabel."

"She's right," Carter said. Hero looked at him with wide eyes. "None of it matters. Adelia has killed more men than I can name in an hour. Retirement doesn't change that."

"I've killed dozens of men," Hero snapped. "So has Houndstooth, and so has Archie. If you think you're in the company of innocents, Carter, you're much mistaken."

"I don't have a warrant for your arrest, or for his," Carter growled back, his finger under Hero's nose, "but if I did—and Archie's neither here nor there, you leave her out of—"

"Pardonnez-moi?" Archie's typically fluting voice was as low and dangerous as the rumble of an approaching avalanche. Carter waved a hand, still towering over Hero.

"You know what I mean," he said.

Archie took a step closer to him, her arms folded across her chest. "Explain it to me, chérie," she said, fury simmering in every word. "Perhaps I do not understand. You know 'ow I *struggle*."

Carter turned to look at her. "I just meant, you know. Once we're married and all, I can't be forced to testify against you, and as long as you don't get yourself into any more trouble . . ."

Hero took a quick step backward as Archie's face went still with cold rage. "'Ow dare you?" Her voice rose with every word. "As long as I don't *get myself into any more trouble*?! As long as I—what was it?" She wheeled on Houndstooth, who threw up his hands in a please-don't-kill-me plea. "As long as I birth a litter of brats and spend my time chasing them away from the fine china, then I can be your wife? As long as I spend all of my time taking care of *you* and *him* and *every fucking one of you useless men*—va te faire enculer! Non," she shouted, turning back to Carter, to Houndstooth's evident relief. "You will marry me as I am, you will love me for who I *am* and for what I am *great* at—or you won't marry me at all, Gran Carter."

"Archie," Carter said, pleading in earnest now, "please, I can't . . . I can't marry a con. I can't marry a killer. I'm a U.S. marshal." He reached for her hands, but she snatched them away. "Please. I've worked my whole life for this star—"

He reached up to tap the star on the brim of his hat, but it wasn't there. Archie shook her head, holding up the stolen star. She'd taken it from his hat without him so much as flinching. "I've worked my 'ole life for this," she said, shaking the star at him. "To be able to do the things that I do—it gives me more than bread, Carter. It gives me *life*. Just like this maudit star gives *you* life. I would never ask you to give this up for me, *never*. And if you think I'll give up my life's work just to marry you, you are not *good enough* for me."

She slapped his star against his chest with enough force to knock him backward a few steps. Adelia closed her eyes over strange, hot tears. *Just finish me,* she thought desperately. *Fight afterward. You'll have time.* When she opened her eyes, Carter was holding both of Archie's hands, murmuring something that sounded like an apology. But before Adelia could get a good read on what he was saying, her view of the fight—or the aftermath, she supposed—was obscured as Hero crouched in front of her.

"Adelia," they said, "I'm not going to kill Burton." Adelia let her head sag, feeling a last trickle hope drain out of her. "But I will get Ysabel back." Adelia looked up. Hero was staring intently into her eyes. "I made you a promise, and I intend to keep it. Do you believe me?"

Adelia nodded without hesitation. She squeezed her eyes shut as another wave of pain washed through her skull, and when she'd opened them, Hero was gone. Archie and Carter startled apart as the door slammed—Houndstooth pushed his way between them, tearing out of the room after Hero.

Carter stared at Adelia, his hand still resting on Archie's arm. The fury in Archie's face seemed to have dimmed, although its ghost was still there, beneath the surface. "How are we going to get her out of here while the party's going on?" Carter murmured.

"It can wait," Archie said. She looked at Adelia with something close to pity. "She's not going anywhere."

Adelia couldn't help agreeing. She was so tired—more tired than she could remember being in a long time. She shifted, rattling the chains again. "Archie," she said, "can I make a request?" When Archie didn't say anything, she decided to go ahead with it. What did she have to lose?

"There are some cabbage leaves on the nightstand there. Please—" She cleared her throat. "Could you please give them to me?"

Archie just stared at her.

"Please? I—what was that?" All three of them looked to the door as another scream rang through the early-evening air.

Carter grabbed Archie's hand. "I promised," he whispered, looking between her and the door. "And I meant it. You're more important to me than—than damn near anything. We'll find a way to make it work. I'm not leaving you again, I promise. I swear, Archie."

"Don't make promises, chérie," Archie murmured back. "Go. I'll watch her," she added with a glance toward Adelia. Carter handed her his key ring, kissed her fiercely, and bolted toward the growing sound of screaming guests. The moment he was gone, Archie grabbed the cabbage leaves and thrust them at Adelia.

"I can't do it myself," Adelia said, rattling the chains.

"What do you need done with them?" Archie asked, massaging her temples.

Adelia told her.

"No," Archie said flatly.

"*Please.*" Adelia felt a flush of shame—she was unaccustomed to begging. "I have had this infection since a few days after Ysabel was taken, and the cabbage leaves are the only thing that's helped. My fever has finally broken, but I don't know if it will come back without—*please,*" she finished weakly.

Archie pursed her lips. "I will not do this for you," she repeated. Then she knelt beside Adelia and, with a rattle of keys, freed her hands. "You will do it for yourself," she continued. "And if you try to run, I will kill you. Is that understood?"

Adelia rubbed her numb wrists in a state of mild shock. "Thank you," she breathed. Archie pressed the cabbage leaves into her hands, then stood at the door with her back to the room.

"What did he say?" Adelia asked, easing her shirt off.

"Hein?" Archie said, turning her back. "What did who say?"

"Carter. What did he say to make you forgive him?"

There was a long pause, long enough that Adelia almost repeated herself. Then, slowly, Archie answered. "I 'aven't forgiven 'im. 'E said all the right things, about respecting me and wanting to find a way that we can both 'ave our lives be what they are supposed to be, and 'ow 'e wasn't thinking straight. So, I've decided to give 'im a chance to prove 'imself. I think that's what love is—it's not about forgiving or forgetting right away. It's about deciding to give someone a chance to earn your forgiveness, eventually."

"And you love him?" Adelia asked.

"More than I know 'ow to express," Archie replied.

"More than the work?"

"No," Archie said. "Not more than the work. But I 'ope there will be a way for me to love them both at the same time. And if there is not—c'est la vie. I will live with 'eartbreak one way or the other."

"We're not so different, I don't think," Adelia ventured as she replaced the old cabbage leaves with the new ones.

Archie barked out a laugh. "We couldn't be more different if our lives depended on it," she said. "But that doesn't mean you deserve to suffer."

"Some people would say it does," Adelia murmured. She examined her swollen breast—it seemed less red than it had even that morning. The pain in her head was pulsing white and grey, but the pain in her breast had eased. *How timely,* she thought. *Perfect.*

"I am not 'some people,'" Archie said. They both went silent, listening to the sound of screams.

"What do you think is going on down there?" Adelia asked. As if to answer her, a bellow cut through the screams like a steam engine bursting through a snowdrift.

Archie spun around to face Adelia, who froze with her shirt half buttoned. Their eyes met, and a terrible knowledge passed between them as another bellow joined the first.

"No," Adelia breathed.

"Ferals," Archie replied. Outside the door to Adelia's quarters, footsteps pounded down the hall. Outside the window, a long, loud scream was cut short by a wet splash.

Chapter 12

HOUNDSTOOTH CAUGHT UP TO Hero just as the first feral rammed into the barge.

"Fuck, fuck, fuck, fuck," they were chanting under their breath as they pushed the doors to the kitchen open. "Fuck, fuck, fuck—" And then, a sound of splintering wood and a bellow of rage blended with the screams of the party guests.

"Hero, wait—" Houndstooth caught Hero under the arms as they stumbled, then immediately stumbled himself. "We have to go," he said as they both found their feet.

"I have to get Ysabel," Hero said.

"No, Hero, we have to *leave,* you don't understand—"

Hero wheeled on him. "Don't tell me what I don't understand," they snapped. "You have no idea what you're talking about. You—I can't talk about this right now. There's no time." They turned back into the kitchen, which was nearly empty save for a sobbing girl with wild red curls and skin so pale that Houndstooth could see a blue vein at her throat. "Hey," Hero snapped their fingers in front of the crying girl's eyes a few times. "You, what's your name? Where's the chef?" When they received no response, they slapped her smartly across the face. The girl's sobs only got louder.

"Where is the chef?" Hero shouted into the girl's face over the sound of bellowing ferals. Houndstooth gripped the doorframe to steady himself as the barge rocked. Hero slapped the girl again.

"Where is the *chef*, tell me!"

The girl shook her head. "She's gone," she cried. "She left when the first feral got here, I'm sorry—"

Another bellow from outside—two, three, and then the barge was rocking again. A pot of something that smelled like damn good she-crab soup fell from the stovetop, spreading a fragrant, steaming slick across the floor.

From somewhere in the kitchen came a high keening sound.

Hero straightened. They let go of the girl, who immediately fled past Houndstooth, slipping on the spill. The noise grew louder, until it sounded like a grinding, grating wail.

Houndstooth realized what was going on just as Hero opened a cupboard and knelt in front of it with a cry of relief.

"Ysabel!" they yelled, reaching into the cupboard to retrieve the swaddled baby.

"How did you—" Houndstooth slipped in the stuff on the floor, catching himself on the oven as a new wave of screams rose outside. "How did you know she'd be in here?"

"The chef sent up cabbage leaves for Adelia," Hero said, clutching the screaming baby to their chest. "That girl with the red hair brought them up. She said that—shhh, Ysabel, hush—they said that the chef had been dealing with an infection like the one Adelia had, just last month." Houndstooth put a hand on their elbow to help them balance as they made their way back to the door. "It was a long shot, but . . . Ysabel had to have a wet nurse. If she hadn't, we would have been able to hear her crying all the way from Port Rouge." Even as they said it, the baby let out a fresh piercing cry. Houndstooth winced.

"We have to leave," Houndstooth said. "Please, Hero—it's not safe, not if the ferals are here."

"I know." Hero bounced Ysabel, and Houndstooth let it go, even if they hadn't been on the Harriet that terrible, blood-soaked morning when the dam collapsed. Even if they couldn't possibly know the danger they were in. "Let's get out of here." They stepped out of the servant's entrance and onto the dock with Houndstooth on their heels.

He watched them run along the dock with Ysabel in

their arms, and he mercilessly crushed the question that rose in his mind—the question of why they hadn't been in touch. Why they'd stayed with Adelia, instead of coming to find him.

He clenched a fist as he tried not to wonder whether they'd missed him at all.

The pond was a horror to survey. Four ferals had found their way into the water—*just four,* Houndstooth thought. *So much chaos for just four.*

Chaos was the only way to describe it. At first glance, Houndstooth thought that all three ferrymen floated on the surface of the water; after a second look, he realized that it was one ferryman floating in three different places. The other two were nowhere to be seen, but the pink tint of the formerly clear water gave him an idea. Their boats had been reduced to splinters in the water; sections of the barge's railing were floating alongside their remains.

Houndstooth looked around Hero, trying to see the paddock, but it was out of sight. *Please,* he thought. *Please let it be whole.* He pushed away a mental image of Ruby, trapped in the paddock as a feral pushed its way in.

He looked back to the water, where a partygoer had seen fit to attempt a swim to shore. The three ferals in the water were still tearing at the severed leg of a ferryman, tossing it into the air as they rammed each other away from it. As Houndstooth watched, the man—blond, and lanky as hell, Houndstooth noted—swam for the shore. He looked over his shoulder at the ferals, who still hadn't noticed him. His eyes were a startling shade of blue.

Houndstooth recognized him with a jolt, and stopped in his tracks, his boots skidding on the wood of the dock.

"Parrish?" he called it out before he realized his error. The swimmer paused, turning to look at who had called out to him.

The ferals looked, too.

"Houndstooth?" The man—Parrish, it was definitely Parrish—was treading water, staring at Houndstooth incredulously.

Houndstooth hadn't believed it until then, not really—hadn't believed that the little blue-eyed boy, the federal agent he'd so deftly exhausted some four months prior, was truly the man behind it all. If Hero hadn't disappeared, Houndstooth realized, he would never have thought of Parrish again.

But Hero *had* disappeared, and somehow this man—the briefest of entertainments in a closed chapter of Houndstooth's life—was back.

"What are you doing here?" Parrish shouted. Houndstooth shook his head, didn't know how to answer. He automatically checked the water, a habit that had hardened over the last few months. He blinked, looked again.

"I'm here for Hero," he said. He went to gesture at Hero—but they were gone, out of sight ahead along the dock.

"Who?" Parrish called, still treading water, his arms making little splashes on the surface of the pond.

"Hero," Houndstooth said. "Hero Shackleby? They came here with Adelia Reyes?"

Parrish spat, looking over the water, his head bobbing as he kicked to keep himself afloat. "This ain't exactly the best time," he said—but he started swimming toward the dock Houndstooth stood on.

Somewhere to Houndstooth's left, Hero's voice called.

"I'm right behind you," he called back, watching Parrish swim.

Watching the water.

"Parrish," he said, not too loudly. "Watch out."

"What was that?" Parrish said, pausing in the water. Footsteps pounded along the dock—Hero was coming back—but Houndstooth couldn't look away from the water.

"I said watch out," he murmured, as four wakes shot along the surface of the water toward Parrish.

"I can't—damn it," Parrish said, pausing in the water, splashing again in an effort to hold still for long enough to hear Houndstooth. His seersucker suit clung to him, and Houndstooth was struck by just how bony the man was. "I can't *hear* you, Houndstooth, what did y—"

And then, just like that, he was gone.

He disappeared below the water with barely a splash—one moment, talking; the next, absent.

Houndstooth counted as Hero drew up short a few feet away. They watched the water with him. *One . . . two . . . three . . . four . . . five*—

And then he was back above the surface, arms thrashing, swimming desperately away from the triangle of ferals that had closed in on him. One surfaced, blood streaming from its drooping, whiskery jowls. Then a second—then a third. They shoved at each other, jaws gaping. Houndstooth spotted a shoe between the teeth of the largest one.

They fought each other and bellowed and Houndstooth half hoped that they'd be too distracted to finish the job. But then Parrish looked back over his shoulder, faltered, took in a lungful of water. He coughed and spat, and the feral with the shoe between its teeth turned.

It saw Parrish.

Parrish screamed as the three ferals, the smaller two closely trailing the largest one, closed in on him. They bumped into each other, snapping and bellowing. Parrish swam as hard and fast as Houndstooth had ever seen a man swim, and it looked as though he might just be able to outswim the ferals.

"No!" A raw scream sounded from the riverboat, and then a girl in a beautiful gown was diving into the water, false curls falling from her head as she jackknifed through the air. Her powerful jump had taken her far, and she entered the water close to Parrish, closer than the ferals. She swam toward him, water frothing before her.

"Acadia," Parrish shouted, choking on water. "Acadia, help—please—"

The girl had reached him, and she grabbed him by the collar, treading water. "Thank God," he gasped, "thank God, you have to help me—"

The girl planted a hand on his head and shoved with a mighty yell. His head disappeared beneath the surface of the water. The girl reached beneath the churn with the hand that wasn't drowning Parrish, and seemed to root around. After a moment, Parrish surfaced, sputtering.

Acadia held up a hand. She was clutching a waxed leather folio.

"No," Parrish said, grabbing for the folio and getting a mouthful of pond water. He was tangled up in his own suit jacket, which had come half off during his struggle. "No, you can't, those are—"

But the girl folded herself in the water, planting both feet on Parrish's shoulders. She pushed off, shoving him down below the surface of the water and springing away from him, and began to swim toward the shore, holding the folio aloft with one hand. And still, the hippos were closing in on Parrish.

He surfaced, choking. He looked after the girl and shouted hoarsely, but she didn't look back. He coughed a few more times before turning to see the trio of ferals approaching, too close for him to even consider escape.

He didn't even have the good sense to drown before they got to him.

Poor bastard, Houndstooth thought. *Three on one? He doesn't stand a—wait.*

He counted the ferals again.

One, two, three.

He could have sworn there had been four before.

The section of the dock that lay between Houndstooth and Hero exploded, shards of wood flying in all directions. Hero stumbled, nearly falling into the water as the dock shook with the force of the feral that was bursting through just a few feet ahead. It bellowed, then vanished below the surface of the water.

Houndstooth watched the shadow in the water as it circled, building momentum for another run at the dock. In front of him, a five-foot section of dock was gone, floating in fragments.

"Hero!" he called, even as he reached over his shoulder to unstrap his harpoon. "Run to the paddock! Abigail is there—"

"I know!" they called back. Houndstooth could only just hear them over the gurgling screams and thick tearing noises coming from the water, where the three ferals had reached Parrish.

And then the fourth feral was back, and Hero was running toward the paddock, and Houndstooth was bracing his feet on the dock although he knew it was a useless effort. He twisted the harpoon in sweat-slick fists, trying to find a grip that would make him feel ready.

The beast burst out of the pond near Houndstooth's feet, spraying water as it bellowed.

Houndstooth aimed the harpoon at the exposed roof of the feral's mouth. As he drove it forward, the feral turned its head to bring its teeth down on his leg. He dodged it so narrowly that he felt whiskers scratch his trouser leg—and then, the harpoon meet soft flesh.

Too soft.

The harpoon was jerked out of his hand, and as he watched, the hippo backed away with the shaft of the harpoon sticking out of from between its teeth like an absurd toothpick. It shook its head, but the harpoon was stuck fast in the back of its throat. Behind Houndstooth, another *thump* shook the dock. He tried to grab the harpoon, but the shaft was already slick with dark blood and the beast was jerking around too quickly for him to get a firm grip.

Something pounded on the dock behind him, hard and fast. Hero was already out of sight ahead of him, and Houndstooth was grateful for that because he wouldn't have wanted them to see him die this way. Sweat soaked his suit jacket, and he peeled it off before rolling up his sleeves. He drew his knife, clenching it between his teeth, and braced his feet on the edge of the dock in preparation. This was it, then: he bent his knees, ready to jump into the water so he could kill the beast in front of him before facing whatever was behind him. He took a deep breath through his teeth, closed his eyes—

"'Oundstooth, *no*!"

He turned as the pounding on the dock behind him got louder, and there was Archie, running toward him with her meteor hammer already swinging. She reached him just as he was stepping back from the dock's edge, and she swung the heavy hammer high before bringing it down with a crunch on the skull of the feral. She dragged it back by the chain, trailing rich red through the water, and wound it up to swing again—but the beast was already sinking below the surface of the water, its skull cracked wide, blood and brain matter floating on the pond's surface like oil.

"Archie—" Houndstooth's heart was pounding in his

ears, and he and Archie stared at each other, breathless. "Where did you *come* from?"

She gestured up toward the second floor of the barge as she wound the chain of the meteor hammer around her waist. "I saw you fighting that thing, and I jumped. Are you alright? Where is 'Ero? 'Ave you seen Carter? What's—"

Houndstooth crushed her in a hug, letting his knife fall to the dock. She embraced him back, clapping him on the shoulder with her free hand.

"You saved my life," he breathed. "Again. God, am I so useless to need all this saving?" She clapped him on the shoulder again, gracious enough to not say *yes*. "Did you see that girl?"

"Who, Acadia?" Archie nodded. "She is . . . formidable, no?"

"Will she be okay?" Houndstooth asked.

Archie laughed. "I think she will be just fine, mon frère. For now, you'll want to worry about yourself."

They both stared at the hole in the dock.

"I don't think I can jump that," Houndstooth said.

"Nor could I," Archie said. "I landed poorly, I am afraid . . . I don't think my ankle could take another landing." Houndstooth looked, and saw that she was standing on one foot. "I think it is not broken, but it will be of no use today."

Behind them, screams rose from the barge as a feral bellowed.

"I don't think we can go back, either," Archie said.

A shadow appeared in the water. "Fucking *damn,*" Houndstooth said. His harpoon was underwater, still clenched in the jaw of the dead feral. He knelt to pick up his knife as Archie hefted her meteor hammer with a weary arm. The shadow stopped in front of him—and without so much as a ripple, Ruby's head slid up out of the water.

"Roo?" he said, disbelieving—but there she was, his Ruby, out of the paddock and ready for him. Her saddle was soaked, but he couldn't begin to care. Behind her, a white splash, and then Rosa's ears flapped above the water's surface.

Houndstooth turned to look at Archie. "Hero must have opened the paddock." As they watched, more shadows filled the water. The ferals, still fighting over the scraps of the swimmer, didn't notice these new hippos until a moment too late—and then the real fight began.

"We 'ave to get out of 'ere," Archie said as the ferals' bellows were met and matched by the roars of the hippos who were attempting to pass them.

"I concur, my friend," Houndstooth said. He held Archie's arm as she stepped down onto Rosa's saddle with her already-swelling ankle.

"Houndstooth!" The call came from around a corner, and then Houndstooth's heart swelled because there was Hero, riding Abigail toward him at breakneck speed. They stopped next to Ruby as Houndstooth settled himself into her saddle, and then the three of them were skirting the frothing knot of ferals and hippos in the center of the pond.

Ruby shook her head and snorted nervously as she swam through the bloodied water. Houndstooth stroked her flank, murmuring to her in an attempt to keep her calm without attracting the attention of the ferals. As they reached the stream that led to Thompson Creek, Carter came running along the bank, one hand pressing his hat to his head.

"Grâce à dieu," Archie breathed—and then she held out a hand and Carter jumped into the saddle behind her, clinging to her waist as they rode away from the fray and into the safe waters of Thompson Creek.

~

They were a few miles down Thompson Creek when Houndstooth asked the question he'd been sitting on since Hero had ridden around the dock on Abigail's back. Archie and Carter rode a hundred feet behind them, squeezed together into one saddle. Rosa was slowed by the extra weight, and Archie had to set an easy pace to keep her ankle free of the stirrups. Houndstooth had been waiting to ask until he and Hero were far enough ahead that he could be certain the sound of his question—and of Hero's answer—wouldn't carry, even over the insect sounds that were rising with the dying light.

"Hero?"

Hero looked at him, and his heart faltered like a hop learning to walk. They looked exhausted, too thin from months doing whatever they'd been doing. Blood and sweat and mud spattered their shirt, and there was a cut on their arm that was too deep not to worry about. They rubbed a hand across their face, smearing the dirt that was smudged there and leaving a light streak across their cheeks.

They were the most magnificent thing he'd ever seen.

"I'm so sorry, Hero." He swallowed around something sharp, something like shame and anger and fear all stuck through his gullet. He was so sorry that he was choking on it. "I should have . . . I'm sorry."

"I'm sorry too," they said.

"What? No—"

"I'm sorry I yelled at you," they continued, as if they hadn't heard him. "I didn't—there was so much happening all at once, and the ferals—"

"It's alright—"

"—and I . . . seeing you, Houndstooth." Their voice broke, and they looked away, but Houndstooth could see starlight reflected in their eyes. "I thought you were dead. I didn't think I'd ever see you again, and I tried not to let myself think about it, but late at night when the baby would cry and wake me up and it would all hit me at once and—"

"Hero—"

"—I'm sorry." It had grown too dark for Houndstooth to see Hero's tears, and he was too far to brush them away with the edge of his thumb.

"It's alright," he murmured. "Or, it's not alright—none of it was alright—but I understand. I'm . . . I thought you were dead, too. The only difference was, instead of pushing the feelings away, I . . ." He paused, struggling to find the words that could describe the depth of his obsession with the idea that Hero *had* to be alive. "I lost myself in them. I said things, Hero. I did things that I didn't have to do. I hurt a man who didn't—he didn't need hurting. I hurt Archie. I hurt her, and I haven't even apologized to her. I don't know if she'll let me."

There was a soft splash as Abigail nudged her shoulder against Ruby's. Houndstooth reached out. He was too far from Hero to lay a hand on their shoulder, but his outstretched fingertips met theirs, if only for a moment.

"I think Archie understands," Hero said. "She knows

what it's like to be far from the person you love."

Houndstooth looked over his shoulder at Archie, Carter, and Rosa, silhouetted in the moonlight. "That she does," he said. He cleared his throat. "Hero, I have to ask you something. I'm sorry, but I just—"

"What is it?" Hero sounded so small in that moment that Houndstooth wanted to cup them in the palm of his hand where they'd be warm. He cleared his throat again and reached out to see if Hero's fingertips were still within reach, but his hand met empty air.

"Houndstooth? What's your question?"

Now or never, he thought. He might as well ask, because the answer would be the same no matter how long he waited.

"I was just wondering," he asked. "Where's Ysabel?"

Chapter 13

HERO DEBATED NOT ANSWERING the question. They were silent for a long time, and Houndstooth, bless him, was patient. He waited while they thought about lying to him, while they thought about ignoring him, while they thought about diving into the water and swimming away.

But in the end, they looked over and, in the dim light of the waning moon, saw him reaching out a hand. He was waiting for their fingertips to meet his—waiting so patiently—and they knew they had no choice but to tell him the truth.

"Adelia has her," they said.

Houndstooth was silent for a long time. Then: "How?"

"She came to the paddock," Hero said. They would never forget the look on Adelia's face when she made it to them. She had burst up out of the water along the edge of the paddock, levering herself over the netting. Hero had asked how she'd dodged the notice of the ferals, but she'd been too out of breath to answer. She'd held out her hands for the baby after scrambling onto the back of a hippo that bore the brand of a Port Rouge rental company. When Hero had handed Ysabel over, Adelia had looked like all of her illness and suffering and flight had been worth it.

"So, what—she's going to keep running?" Houndstooth's voice was gentle, and Hero couldn't hold back their smile.

"Well. I was going to talk to you about that."

Hero leaned forward to rub Abigail between the ears, remembering the sight of Adelia on her stolen hippo, fading into the shaded section of the paddock, as shadowy as Ruby in the water. She had been looking down at Ysabel with tears streaming down her face. Hero reached into their pocket and felt the smooth stone that rested there—a stone plucked from the bank of Thompson Creek, if they had to guess. With their thumb, they could almost feel the image that was etched into the stone. Two hippos, shoulder to shoulder.

"Goodbye, Hero."

"Goodbye?"

"This is the 'end of the line,' no?" Adelia hadn't sounded bitter in the slightest as she repeated Hero's words back to them.

"I—well, I don't—"

"It's alright, Hero," Adelia had said, her lips brushing Ysabel's hair. "It's what we agreed. You would help me find Ysabel, and then we would part ways."

Hero had done many brave things in their life. They

drew on all the courage they possessed. "Adelia, what if—Houndstooth and I. We're going to start a ranch. We haven't talked about it since before the Harriet, obviously, but . . ."

"But you know he has not changed his mind about it," Adelia had said, stroking Ysabel's wispy hair.

"I haven't changed mine," Hero had replied. "And back before everything happened, we talked about it, he and I, and we were going to do it. I have my land, and now we have the capital from the Harriet job."

Adelia had been silent, absorbed in Ysabel. The green shadows of the paddock had fallen across her face, and Hero had felt a bone-deep certainty that they might never see her again.

"I was thinking," Hero said, a tremor in their voice. "We'll need a ranch hand. Someone who knows their way around. Someone who we can trust." Adelia's silence had thickened then, had solidified into something taut and patient. Hero had waited.

"It would not be a good life for Ysabel, running and hiding all the time," Adelia had finally said. "It would be good for her to grow up on a ranch. Around people who aren't killers."

"We're all killers," Hero murmured. "But we'd love her like family."

Adelia had looked up then, a slant of dappled light illuminating her wet face. "Like family," she'd said, and there had been something like a smile in her voice.

"Anyway. It'll take us a month or so to get there," they'd said, awkwardly rubbing the back of their neck. "And we'll have to do some work on Carter in the meantime, convincing him not to go get a new warrant for you and all. But maybe you can meet us there . . . ?"

"Maybe I can," Adelia had said. And then Ysabel had begun to stir, and a horrible scream had sounded from the pond, and they'd all had to leave, and Hero hadn't been sure if "maybe" meant "I'll never see you again"—not until they'd found that stone in their pocket.

"I was going to talk to you about that," Hero said again, and Houndstooth looked over at them. "But maybe it can wait until morning."

"Maybe it can," Houndstooth said. The silence between them was quickly devoured by the night-bugs and the soft splashes of Ruby and Abigail moving through the water.

Hero took their hand out of their pocket and, at last, reached toward Houndstooth. Houndstooth's fingers found theirs, and they rode like that for a time—fingers just touching, Ruby's and Abigail's shoulders pressed close. Just enough to remind each other that they were together in the dark, until they could look at each other in the light.

Acknowledgments

Thank you so much to DongWon Song and Justin Landon, who thought that I wrote something worth publishing, and who made it better at every turn. Thanks also to the tireless team of beta readers and sensitivity readers who told me where I was going wrong, and without whom none of this would have happened. Special love and appreciation to the Murder Friends and PQ, who support me through my endless flailing; to the cabin-retreat crew, who know that Pepper is a Dog; and to Geoff, for bringing wine when the chapters got hard to write. I couldn't do any of it without you.

About the Author

Photograph by Raj Anand

Hugo and Campbell finalist **SARAH GAILEY** came onto the scene in 2015 and has since become one of the sharpest, funniest voices in pop culture online. She is a regular contributor for multiple websites, including *Tor.com*. Her nonfiction has appeared in *Mashable* and the *Boston Globe,* and her fiction has been published internationally. She has a novel forthcoming from Tor Books in Spring 2019. She lives in Oakland, California.

TOR·COM

Science fiction. Fantasy. The universe.

And related subjects.

*

More than just a publisher's website, *Tor.com* is a venue for **original fiction, comics,** and **discussion** of the entire field of SF and fantasy, in all media and from all sources. Visit our site today—and join the conversation yourself.